THIS OTHER EDEN

THREE STORIES AND THREE NOVELLAS

By Michael Hemmingson

Dybbuk Press

New York, NY

http://www.dybbuk-press.com

Published by Dybbuk Press, First Edition, May 2010.

Library of Congress Control Number: 2009923951
ISBN: 0-9766546-6-0
13 digit ISBN: 978-09766546-67

Acknowledgements

"That Never Happened" was originally published as "This Other Eden" in *Gargoyle* #48 (2005) edited by Richard Peabody. It was also published in Japan in the magazine *Subaru* (Feb. 2006).

"Where He Was the Day it Happened" was originally published as "Tuck" in The *Urban Bizarre*, edited by Nick Mamatas (Prime Books, 2004). It was also published in Japan in the journal *Panic Americana* #7 (2005) edited by Takayuki Tatsumi.

"What Happens Between Literary Agents and Clients While in New York" was originally published as "The Agent" in *Tempting Desire* (Two Backed Books, 2005) edited by Jon Edward Lawson. It was also the basis for a pilot teleplay by the same name, optioned by Fox 21 in 2007 but never developed, and probably never will be.

"And Then It Happened" first appeared as an e-book from Amazon Shorts (2007). An excerpt appeared in *Fiction International* (2005) edited by Harold Jaffe.

Advanced Praise for This Other Eden

"Both humorous and profound, Hemmingson's new collection calls humanity on the carpet and makes us all account for our sins. A brilliant and refreshing collection of stories from an equally brilliant and refreshing author."

~ Ronald Damien Malfi, author of *Passenger*

Provocative and intriguing, THIS OTHER EDEN by Michael Hemmingson is akin to reading a cross between someone's private journal and a True Crime magazine. Feeling titillated and naughty, as if reading a sibling's most private and dirty secrets, I found myself wholly unwilling to put this book down. It is glorious train wreck of loss, betrayal, and crime mixed with intimate thoughts and a poignant sense of loneliness. THIS OTHER EDEN is the kind of book that will make you forget your own life for a while but will also allow you to be grateful for it when you put the book down.

~ Jennifer Brozek, Submissions Editor, Apex Book Company

Praise for previous Hemmingson works

"...the master of the avant-pop genre...an oddly twisted brand of sin and redemption."

-American Book Review, on *Nice Little Shorties Jam-Packed with Depraved Sex and Violence*

"Hemmingson's writing skips from realism to fable and through time and space...His confident imagination [is] borderline sadistic and playful."

–San Diego Union-Tribune, on the play, *Driving Somewhere*

"Hemmingson is Raymond Carver on acid."

–Larry McCaffery, editor of *Avant-Pop: Fiction for a Daydream Nation*

"This writer should be turned into the police and incarcerated."

–An anonymous peer reviewer at an academic journal, commenting on one of Hemmingson's essays.

CONTENTS

Nothing Like That Ever Happened   9

What Happens when Things Happen to People   19

Where He was the Day It Happened   77

Now That I Know What Happened, Could You   85
Hold Me, Please, and Say This is Love?

What Happens Between Literary Agents and   161
Clients While in New York

And Then It Happened   175

With your Language, You are looking for a New Heart.

---Gordon Lish

Nothing Like That Ever Happened

I met my daughter's mother in the spring quarter Comparative Literature course that I was guest teaching. I was thirty-two and filled with delusions about writing the great American novel. You know the type: unpublished and inevitably unpublishable.

The young woman's name was Pauline and this is the first thing she thought when she saw me: *I will marry that man*. She was nineteen. She was twenty when she gave birth to Gillian.

We lived a simple and destitute life in a one-bedroom apartment two blocks from campus. Pauline was still working on graduating and I was jumping from job to job like a true bum. Sometimes the university hired me for guest teaching spots when they couldn't find anyone else. I worked at pizza parlors, gas stations, used bookstore; all the time laboring on my novel that was close to 700 pages long when I realized I'd never finish it. It was going nowhere and it was, ultimately, bad.

Gillian wrote her first novel when she was five. It was a short book, 130 pages long, and while it didn't see print until after her sixth, it still stands as something remarkable: a very adult-sounding product penned from the hand of a child.

My daughter published her first novel when she was nine-years-old. It was the third she'd written.

I imagine some of your jaws dropping, but this isn't unheard of. Taylor Caldwell started publishing books when she was Gillian's age.

Read Steven Millhauser's *Edwin Mullhouse*.

You may ask: how did I, an unpublished novelist who'd just turned forty, feel about my daughter doing such a thing? You would think that I would be jealous, flabbergasted; that it would destroy my ambitions and notions. Well, I'd long given up on my dreams when Gillian's first novel came out; I'd convinced myself I was the better for it. And this publication wasn't any surprise;

Pauline and I were proud parents. We both knew something like this would happen; maybe not so soon, but eventually. Gillian grew up with books. Her mother read books to her when she was in the womb. Books were everywhere in our cramped apartment— every wall towered with shelves. Volumes were jammed in closets, under tables, in the kitchen and bathroom. Gillian had the vocabulary of a ten-year-old when she was eighteen months; she began scribbling stories and poems in a notebook at four. For her eighth birthday, my wife and I gave her a laptop; that's when she began the novel that would be published a year later, *The Royal Throne of Kings,* an 110,000 word tale of precocious children in a big city, set in what is best called an alternate universe

She derived the title from Shakespeare, as she would all her subsequent books. Pauline and I took Gillian to plays; Gillian was for reasons unknown to me drawn to a production of *Richard II* that she saw at age seven. The next day, Gillian found a copy of the play in the library and read it that night. She wrote out, in block letters on construction paper, a passage. She taped it to her wall; it remained there for years:

> *This royal throne of kings, this scepter'd Isle,*
> *This earth of majesty, this seat of Mars,*
> *This other eden, demi-paradise,*
> *This fortress built by Nature for herself*

I can't put my finger on why these particular words inveigled her, but when she titled her second novel *The Sceptered Isle* and her third *The Earth of Majesty,* I had a pretty good idea what her subsequent books would be called.

The matter of how my daughter Gillian published her first novel is one of those wonderful stories that young unpublished writers (and some old ones) love to hear but in their hearts know must be myth, because no one is ever that lucky.

Well, this is true.

One of Pauline's friends from college went to New York after graduation and became an editor at a commercial publishing conglomerate. She came home one Christmas and dropped by. Of course, Pauline proudly informed her old classmate, whose name was Nancy, that her young daughter was a writer with three novel-length manuscripts.

"Are you kidding me?" said Nancy.

"No," said Pauline.

"And she's *eight?*" said Nancy.

"She'll be nine soon," I said.

"Can I ask you this," said Nancy, "can I ask to see one of these manuscripts? I'd be very interested in reading one."

Pauline said, "Well, I don't think Gillian would mind," and I knew that this was my wife's plan from the start. She didn't believe anything would come of this; she probably thought Nancy would be impressed and wonderstruck, certainly not making the phone call that came six days later.

"I read *The Royal Throne of Kings* on the flight back," Nancy said, "and two other people here have looked at it and well - well, we'd like to make an offer to publish it. Obviously, we can market this book because of the author's age, the novelty alone will get attention, but moreover; this is a remarkably well-written novel. I was moved, very moved, and that happens so infrequently, believe me. But before we go any further, for everyone's protection all around, you should get an agent for Gillian. She has two other books, right? Yes, you should get an agent for her. I know this agent, a very good agent, a very prominent one."

The agent's name was Samantha Cartwright. She represented, I found out later, many of my favorite contemporary writers. Ms. Cartwright wanted to meet Gillian in the flesh, so

Pauline and I flew out to New York with Gillian who, I might add, was receiving a $25,000 advance for *The Royal Throne of Kings*.

We met Cartwright in her office on the eleventh floor of a tall skinny building. Location: Park Avenue South. She was a smartly dressed woman in her late forties.

She said, "Let me tell you, I've never gotten used to repping the current wunderkinden of American letters; these twenty-three-year-olds walking out of MFA programs with gems of flawed young novels; these twenty-year-olds that come out of nowhere with their one-hit razzle-dazzles. But a nine year old? This I wasn't ready for. Sheesh, Nancy has sent me a doozy. Tell me, Gillian, are you prepared for fame?"

"I guess so," Gillian said softly, staring at the floor.

"Don't be so shy," Cartwright said.

"She usually isn't," said Pauline.

"Tell me, Gillian, how many more novels do you have in that smart little head of yours?"

"Many," Gillian replied. "A lot."

"I hope so."

***

Fame didn't come to Gillian with that first book, but there were hints of it. *The Royal Throne of Kings* received a lot of critical attention, good and bad; the sales in hardback were modest, but it did better in paperback, along with the hardcover edition of *The Sceptered Isle*.

Gillian was fourteen when *The Earth of Majesty* entered the world and several bestseller lists. By this time, Pauline had left us both and filed for a divorce.

I mentioned that my daughter's curious success did not bruise my ego, and this is true. I was behind her career one hundred and ten percent; I was her loudest cheerleader, her greatest fan. I guess you can say I experienced literary fame vicariously. This wasn't the same for Pauline.

My wife didn't have artistic aspirations. She was an academic. When she overhead a fellow instructor at the community college refer to her as 'the mother of that literary freak' it dawned on her what, truly, an anomaly our child was.

"Don't you think," she asked me, "that this is just too odd? One or two novels maybe, but a whole bunch of them? My God, she's been talking about a septet she wants to complete before she's twenty-one!"

"Mozart," I said, "Beethoven."

"Frankenstein," she said.

"We created something beautiful, Pauline."

"Too beautiful."

She eventually left her husband and daughter. She had been offered a tenured-track job at a big university several states away. There was also a man she was sleeping with, a faculty member at said university. Was I hurt? Of course. Was I surprised? Not at all. We hadn't made love in more than a year.

***

Gillian was on the bestseller lists. My ex-wife was making a new home with her academic lover, and I was alone, sitting in my chair and watching everything. Like the song says, "How did I get here?" If Gillian was ever troubled or pained about her mother's departure, she didn't reveal it. For the next three years, she worked every day on her 700 page science-fictional tome, *The Seat of Mars*. She was seventeen when the work hit the bookstores; it was a success. By this time, she was attending Yale; admitted early.

The day she was accepted, Gillian showed me a surprising gesture of affection. She came into my room and sat on the edge of the bed and said, "Daddy, I won't go if you don't want me to."

13

"What are you saying?"

"Yale. You'll be all alone here. I don't want you to be alone."

"I'm used to being alone," I said. "You're not going to pass this up."

"I don't need school, really."

"Nonsense," I said.

She got under the covers and said, "Will you hold me like when I was little?"

I held her. She cried. I didn't ask why she was crying. I didn't want her to know how much I'd actually miss her.

So off she went.

***

I realize I'm breezing through a lot of years and life here, but there really isn't anything to say about the time. What I really want to get at is the publication of Gillian's fifth novel, *The Other Eden*. At 450 pages, critics called it her most autobiographical work to date; a matter that upset me greatly.

The novel is narrated by a character named Gwendolyn, the only one of Gillian's books composed in the first-person. Gwendolyn is a child-genius, a master of the piano performing in concerts at the age of seven. Her mother dies when she's ten, and over the years, as she becomes more known for her piano work (composing and recording original scores), another aspect of her life remains dark and secret: an incestuous relationship with her father. Fifty years old, a former rock musician, her father is a recluse: he never dates, he never goes out. *There was never any force involved*, stated the end of Part One, Chapter Nine, *it was a mutual connection between two sad and lonely human beings who had lost someone they dearly loved.*

The first phone call about it came from Pauline.

"I want to talk to you about Gillian's new novel," she said.

"All right," I said.

"Is any of it true? Were you having sex with her?"

"Jesus Christ, of course not," I said.

"Then why did she write that stuff?"

"I have no idea."

"The whole novel...*that's our lives*. And she *killed me*. Is that what she thinks of me? Does she hate me? Does she wish I died instead of running away?"

"She loves you," I said, although I didn't know if this were true.

"If I find out," Pauline said, "if I find out that you two…"

"Nothing like that ever happened," I said. "I can't believe you'd even entertain the…"

"You were both so close."

"I won't listen to your accusations."

"Maybe she's mad," said Pauline.

"Maybe she's completely insane," she said.

***

I met Gillian at a seafood restaurant in New Haven.

"You haven't had lobster until you've eaten there, Daddy," she said.

She was right. The food was wonderful.

You can imagine that I had a hard time enjoying it, though. I was here on a mission. I was here to find out why she'd written such a book. I drank. I figured if I had enough drinks I could build up the courage to confront her.

It wasn't easy. She wasn't the Gillian I once knew - she wasn't a small girl sitting across from me. She was a grown woman and a successful novelist.

"How did you like your dinner?" she asked.

"It was very good," I said.

"I'm glad," she said, taking a credit card out of her purse.

"I won't let you pay for dinner," I said.

"I insist," she said.

I noticed she had a platinum Visa.

After dinner, we went for a walk.

"Gillian," I said.

"Daddy," she said.

"Gillian, listen," I said, "listen to me, I came here - I wanted to - I came here to. Look," I said, "it's about your new book."

"I know," she said. "I was wondering when that would come up. I could tell it was on your mind. I knew this was bound to happen sooner or later."

She stopped and sat down on a bench. I sat next to her. She looked at the ground. There were a lot of dead leaves on the ground.

"Why?" I said. "Why did you write that thing?"

"Why does any writer write anything?"

"People are talking," I said. "Your own mother - "

"She called me."

"She did?"

"Oh she did."

"What did you say?"

"I told her the book meant nothing."

"People think the book is about us," I said.

"They do?" she said.

"Yes," I said.

"Let them think what they want," she said.

"People think you and I," but I couldn't say it.

"Are you ashamed?" she said.

"I don't want people to think that."

"What if it were true?" she said. "It happened to Anaïs Nin. It's happened to many - Dorothy Allison and…"

"What are you *saying?*"

"Before I left for Yale," she said, "I came to you, I was in bed with you - are you telling me - are you telling me you don't remember?"

"Nothing happened," I said softly.

"And the other times? Before?"

I started crying. *"Nothing* like that ever happened between us, Gillian."

"But what if I *wanted* it to happen?" she said. "What if *you* wanted it to? If we both did? Isn't that just like - if it did happen?"

I wept. "Why are you doing this?"

She grabbed my arm and told me to hush. "All right, all right," she said. "It never happened."

I asked, *"Why* did you write that book?"

"It's just a *book*, Daddy," she said, "just fiction."

WHAT HAPPENS WHEN
THINGS HAPPEN TO PEOPLE

...he felt...as if he were supposed to be doing something else, something grander, higher, more difficult, more dangerous, more daring.

—Steven Millhauser, *Martin Dressler*

IVY'S BEAUTIFUL SKIN

On their second date, Edmond and Ivy experienced a prejudice they would learn to ignore. They were in line to see a movie, and someone said, "Hey, man, why are you with a nigger?"

Edmond wanted to fight the guy. Ivy took his arm and said, "Forget it. What do you expect from stupid people?"

She had a point.

"Nigger lover," someone else said.

"That's right!" Ivy said, laughing. "Don't you wish you could have a piece of my sweet black ass?"

Ivy had experienced this sort of thing all her life (she was twenty-four) because her father was white and her mother black; her skin was light brown, the most beautiful skin Edmond had ever seen. He met her at one of those quickie $8 haircut stores; she was renting a booth and working too many hours to pay the rent and her tuition at San Diego State University. Edmond walked in to get an $8 cut. He gave Ivy a $20 bill and had said, "Keep the change."

"That's quite a tip," Ivy had said. "I can't take a $12 tip."

"Why not?"

"Well."

"Look, I don't do this sort of thing."

"Tip big?"

"Ask strangers out."

"Strangers? I just cut your hair. Me and your scalp are quite intimate."

"I'm sorry," he'd said, feeling like he'd just made a fool of himself. He never knew how to ask women for dates. It was always awkward. He started to go. Ivy stopped him.

"Hey."

"Yeah."

"Where you heading?"

"I don't know."

"You were asking me out."

"I was."

"So, take me out. Take me out to lunch. Out to the ball game. Out of *here*."

"Today?"

"Sure."

"When's your lunch break?"

"Now," she'd said. "I'm an independent subcontractor, I don't punch in a time clock."

Later, she would tell Edmond that she was attracted to him the moment he sat in her chair, and if he hadn't made the first move, she would have. (He didn't believe her.) She would tell him, "You and I, we're destiny; it's in the stars that we'll have an interesting life together."

So, when people made comments or gave them looks in public, Edmond learned to ignore these abuses of language and propriety.

THE APPLE

Ivy decided they needed to leave San Diego. She was done with college; she had an M.A. and she wanted to be an editor at a publishing company. That meant going to New York.

Edmond shrugged and said, "Sure." He didn't think she was serious, but oh she was. They didn't move immediately, it took them almost a year to get there. They had to save money. Ivy worked extra hours at the hair store; she even started cutting hair at the apartment. She didn't spend a dime on unnecessary things. The two hardly went out to dinner or movies; everything went into the bank for 'The Big Apple Transfer.'

Edmond worked in a variety of odd and unrewarding jobs. He cooked and delivered pizzas, he pumped gas and he hammered nails into wood - nothing he was good at. When Christmas time came, he got a job at a big toy store conglomerate stocking the overhead product and filling the shelves with dolls. He was good at it; in fact, management asked him to stay on as a permanent employee. He worked at the toy store 9-5, five days a week and one Sunday a month; one splendid morning Ivy woke up and said, "We have enough money in the bank, let's go."

"Right now?"

"Start packing."

"Okay."

Two days later they rented a moving truck. The truck cost a third of their savings.

They had no great adventure moving across America; when they stopped to buy gas or eat, every place looked identical and no one (as they feared) gave them trouble for being an interracial couple. Edmond had it all mapped out in his mind, like the movies. Some trucker stop, evil truckers talking about ebony and ivory, pinching Ivy's butt, hitting him in the face and then there would be the inevitable violence and that sad, if not ironic, end to their young lives and goals.

Ivy's goals. He was a day-to-day guy and his girlfriend had the prerequisite visions of grandeur; taking New York by storm, becoming important and famous. New York. He liked the feel of the city—the smell, the people, the buildings, the weather.

His mother told him he made a mistake.

"New York is a cesspool," she said on the phone after he called to inform her of the move, "What were you thinking? Are you crazy? You're living there with that girl? What's her name? Blossom?"

"Ivy."

"Poison. This is *her* idea, right?"

"We're happy, Mom."

"No you're *not.*"

"We're fine."

"You're *poor.*"

"We'll get by."

"You'll regret this decision, I just know it."

"I did the right thing."

"Edmond, come back home."

"Stop *worrying*, Mom."

"What about your *future?*"

"It's the future," he said.

IVY MEETS THE LARGER-THAN-LIFE ALONZO CREWS & BEGINS HER CAREER IN PUBLISHING

For half a year, Ivy applied to all the publishing companies and magazines in town. She never got a single call-back. It depressed her but she kept at it. "It just takes time," she told herself each day, "it takes time." She covertly wrote very short stories and even shorter poems; this was such a secret she didn't even tell Edmond. If she told him, he might want to read her tiny stories and poems and then what would he think? Most of them were about sex - not real sex, but imaginary and often bizarre encounters people would have with strangers or animals and odd other-worldly creatures. She enjoyed writing in notebooks; when Edmond was asleep or she was in a coffeeshop she would open the notebook and write with a number two pencil. The subway would suffice for composing five-line poems. When Edmond was gone, she would type her writings up on her 1970s Olympia manual and (so they wouldn't be around and mistakenly discovered) she would send the things off to magazines and literary journals.

One such journal with a post office box address in Brooklyn, *The Peach*, sent her encouraging words. *Very dandy*, the handwritten rejection notes said, *quite intriguing, this tickled my fancy but didn't fancy me enough, oh this one was close! Send more! Yes, my dear, yes, send more!* Ivy sent more. The rejection notes remained encouraging: *Keep sending! Keep sending! Please know that I know what you're doing, what you want to do, that Alonzo is keeping watch, Alonzo watches with interest*, and *Alonzo wants you to send more, to send all you have*.

The editor of *The Peach* was Alonzo Crews. One day he called Ivy on the phone. He said, "Ms. Gaylord, Ms. Gaylord, is that you, Ms. Gaylord?" He had a singsong and scratchy voice.

"Yes," she said cautiously.

"Alonzo Crews here."

"Oh yes," she said.

"I've decided you need my help. Yes, this is what I have decided. I like what you're doing, but you're not quite there. You need guidance. You should take my class."

"Class?"

"I hold a private writing class, a session every four months, a tri-quarterly affair. You belong there."

"I don't know what to say."

"You should say yes. Yes, say *yes*, and *learn.*"

She had to think about it because the price of the class was far from cheap. She had just enough in the bank, but that would mean she and Edmond would have to live frugally for a while.

That week, Ivy finally got a job interview at a publishing company. During the interview (it was a proofreading position) she mentioned that a fellow named Alonzo Crews suggested she take his class. The managing editor, a pale and balding gentleman who looked too skinny for his baggy clothes, dropped his jaw and opened his eyes very wide and said, "Are you *serious? The* Alonzo Crews?"

"You've heard of him?"

"Who *hasn't?"*

"He has this magazine—"

"People beg and bribe to be in his class. Many big writers have been students under him. If he asked you, consider yourself among the chosen."

"I didn't know."

"You haven't lived in New York long enough."

She nodded. "I have much to learn."

"You'll learn a lot from the man, I'm sure."

"So you think I should take the class?"

"You shouldn't be thinking twice."

"It's a lot of money."

"Take out a bank loan."

"A job would help."

"It's just proofreading and we don't publish fiction here. We publish science and psychology."

"I *love* those subjects."

"Can you start Monday?"

"Bright and early."

"Welcome aboard then."

There was much to celebrate. She bought two bottles of champagne on the way home. She called the phone number *The Peach's* editor had given to her.

"Yeah."

"Is Alonzo Peach—I mean, Alonzo Crews there?" She was excited; she knew it was him on the phone—*that voice.*

"He is here."

"Mr. Crews?"

"He is here."

"This is Ivy Gaylord."

24

"Yes, yes—of course, yes. What can Alonzo do for you, dear?"

"I'll enroll in your class."

"There is no 'enrollment.' You're either there, or you're somewhere else. And there are no refunds."

"Well then," she said, "I want to be there."

"Good, good. I knew you would."

"Thank you."

"Don't thank me yet," he said, "you haven't been in my class."

When Edmond came home, carrying a pizza and smelling like pizza, because he was working in a pizza joint, she said, "I'm tired of pizza, honey."

"It's free," he said.

She showed him the champagne bottles.

"What's this?"

It was time to come clean, to reveal her secret. She told him about the job, and then the writing, *The Peach*, the class, how the man's name probably got her the job. He hugged her. He said he was happy. He said he knew about her clandestine literature.

"We've been together long enough," Edmond said. "How could I not know?"

She said, "Oh."

He said he was wondering when she'd tell him.

"Now you know," Ivy said. "Let's make a pact, here and now."

"Okay."

"No secrets between us, ever. Wait."

They opened a bottle and poured champagne into paper cups.

She held up her cup.

"No secrets, ever."

Alonzo Crews' class proved to be elucidating and gruesome; not just the class, but the man. He was six feet tall, robust, and wore an orange jumpsuit with a white T-shirt. He looked like a prison inmate. He thrived on his eccentricity. He had swarthy skin, green eyes, and long black hair that he always kept in a pony tail. He moved his hands when he talked and he talked a lot. The man loved to hear his own voice. The twice-a-week class (Mondays and Wednesdays, six p.m. until late, sometimes one or two in the morning) was held at an on apartment in the West Village. This was not Crews' home; he lived in 'the heart of the heart of Brooklyn, where my heart of hearts lives and dies.' The apartment, he explained, "belongs to an old, dear, and trusted friend. Someone I once nurtured, whom I give a fifteen percent cut of the money you pay for this use. This is the apartment of someone famous, perhaps quasi-famous, perhaps someone whose books you may have read. But I will not give out her name, for she has requested anonymity. Nonetheless, here we are in this cozy little abode with walls lined with books, and here I will teach all you rascals how to create great sentences." He rattled off names of writers, known and obscure, whom he had a hand in publishing.

"Yes," he said, "I used to be an editor at a very fine, very refined literary publishing house, where for years I acquired and edited many books; alas, said genteel house was purchased by a multinational conglomerate and the new owners did not see, shall we say, eye-to-eye with Alonzo's view of American letters; thus Alonzo said, 'Fare thee well, adieu, so long, and kiss my wrinkled arse' and faded into semi-retirement and the publication of *The Peach*. Why *The Peach* you ask? Because the work I publish in those humble pages are peachy-keen."

Crews was a ruthless critic and teacher. He tore apart every single sentence Ivy, or anyone else in the class, wrote.

"Would you die for that sentence?" he'd say. "If you're not willing to die for every sentence you compose, then kill the

26

sentence! Or kill yourself and be done with it! Or walk out of here and forget about being a writer! Don't sit there and cry. *Die!* Die or have your sentences save your life!"

He frightened some away; the class started with fifteen, and three weeks later, seven remained.

"Now," Crews said, "we're nice and small and can really begin to learn."

Ivy almost didn't make it. She wanted to quit the first night after Crews dismantled the first two paragraphs of one of her stories. It was a five page piece, but she couldn't get past page one without Crews saying, "No, no, no, shit shit shit."

Edmond told her she could not give up so fast.

"I won't take such abuse," Ivy said.

"You can't get your money back."

"It sucks," she said.

"It sounds to me like he's weeding out the weak from the strong. I know you, you're strong. This is what you want. It's what you need. Everyone here is a hard-ass. You have to be just as hard."

She stayed. She followed Crews' advice, she wrote the way he wanted people to write, and she liked the product. Near the end of the class, Crews allowed her to finish reading her stories out loud with few comments.

"That's very good," he'd say, "Those are the kind of words and sentences that make my dick hard."

He asked Ivy if he could buy her a cup of coffee.

"It's eleven-thirty at night," she said.

"It'll be weak coffee."

They went to a place in the Village, a nice place as Crews described it; an all-night diner where people could be alone to sit and talk, "to plan, to scheme, to rejoice and lament," said Crews.

"What a reputation to live up to," said Ivy, "for such a common little diner."

"I've been meaning to do this for some weeks now."

"Do what?"

"Find out about Ivy; who she is, where she comes from, where she's going. These things interest Alonzo very much."

She thought it was strange to be in public with a man who wore an orange jumpsuit; she expected looks. No one in the diner seemed to notice. She didn't have the nerve to ask him about his clothing, so she asked, "Why do you sometimes refer to yourself in the third person?"

He said, "I have no idea what you're talking about. This is a good cup of coffee. It's amazingly hard to find a decent, good - *good* - cup of ordinary, simple American coffee. Why is this? We're losing the simple things more and more, every day, and we're not even aware of it. Drink your coffee."

Ivy barely sipped; she was not interested in coffee. She wanted to know what Crews was up to. She caught him staring at her tits. She didn't want to play games. She wanted to get this over with.

"You're from California."

She said, "Yes."

"San Francisco, perhaps? I've had seminars there. I know people there. The City Lights Bookstore is there. Let me tell you about San Francisco; when I was younger, when I was your age, maybe even younger than you, when I was living in Bozeman, Montana - did I ever mention this is where Alonzo once resided? Bozeman! But he was born, I was born in New Mexico. Roswell, where the UFO crashed. After the UFO crashed, my parents packed up and we moved to Montana. Anyway, San Francisco. After I read *On the Road*, I wanted to go there and find Dean Moriority: befriend him, travel with him, drink bottles of wine and smoke reefer with him."

"He's a fictional character."

"I was a very stupid young man."

"You were naïve."

28

"I was dumb."

"San Francisco is nice," Ivy said, "but I'm from San Diego."

"Ah, ah. Have I been there? Yes, Alonzo has. Oops, there goes that rotten third person again. I believe I stayed at the Hotel del Coronado once or twice. A splendid, wonderful and opulent place."

"I've never been."

"So you moved East."

"Yes."

"Seeking the literary life."

Ivy couldn't look at him. "Yes."

"It's a noble cause," Crews said.

"I think so," she said.

"You came alone?"

"I packed up the boyfriend too."

"There's *always* a boyfriend."

"A girl can't be alone."

"No, no, alone is never good. People need people, like the song says."

"His name is Edmond."

"A solid, sturdy name."

"We live in a very small, very crappy place on 4th Avenue."

"I know many people in the Lower East."

"You know many people everywhere, I take it."

"Yes, I do."

"We don't have a lot of money," Ivy said. "We stayed in a crappy motel when we first got here, we stayed there for almost three weeks and I hated it. Our apartment isn't much better, but at least it's our apartment. It's what we call home."

"He's an aspiring novelist, perhaps?"

That made Ivy laugh.

"Hardly. He isn't an aspiring anything. I don't know what Edmond wants to do with his life. He's still…finding himself. I

29

guess. He likes to take pictures. He likes his camera. It's nothing he's very serious about. What does he do? He flips the dough."

"What?"

"He makes pizzas."

"I dread pizza."

"I used to love it. Now he brings pizza home all the time."

"Maybe he'll open his own pizza store."

"I hope not. I'll leave him," she laughed.

"This is serious?"

"I love him."

"He flips the dough good?"

"He flips *very* good," she said.

"Your writing," Crews said, leaning back. "You're serious about it, I know, but not serious enough."

"What do you mean?"

"Your heart of hearts lies somewhere else."

"You're wise, Alonzo," and she told him about her proofreading job, how she had tried to get into publishing ever since arriving to Manhattan.

He nodded. He said, "An editor."

She said, "Yes."

He said, "Tell me more about Edmond. How did you meet? When did you realize you were in love?"

"No, tell *me* about Alonzo," Ivy said. "I've said enough. You're the talker, so talk."

Crews sipped his coffee.

"Where to begin? There's always a beginning, but not where you might think. Roswell, the alien spaceship, Bozeman. Montana is a beautiful place, you should go there sometime; believe me, believe you me, you will not be disappointed. I don't mean you should move there and live there. You are not a woman who would be happy living in Bozeman, but you would be enlightened by a visit. I could have been a cowboy; somewhere in my heart of hearts, there is a cowboy. I never let that cowboy out. Like you, I came to New York to live a glamorous literary life. The vision: I would dine at Elaine's and hobnob with Capote and Plimpton. I was still naïve, as you say, as you can imagine. But Alonzo had dreams, yes he did, and although, like yourself, he met many closed doors when trying to find a job in publishing, he was determined as all holy hell. So what did he do? What did I do? He began a literary magazine. *The Apple*. Called *The Apple*. 'Why *The Apple*?' Ivy Gaylord asks. Because the magazine was the apple of my eye. Every story and poem Alonzo published was the apple of his fine eye. And it was a *good* magazine, publishing *good* work, enticing submissions from *good* names of *good* literature. And so, New York publishing took notice of Alonzo Crews. 'Oh, here's the man who publishes that *good* magazine.' Indeed, Alonzo found a job editing books at a good company and he stopped publishing *The Apple*. After thirteen fine issues, *The Apple* was no more. Books became Alonzo's passion, and for a dozen years he edited many, many fine books. Some of them are taught in schools all over the world. 'Why?' Because they are instant classics, they are books that will endure the test of time and whatnot. Somewhere along the line, Alonzo married a *very good* woman, Diana. Diana used to write short fiction, such as yourself, but the passion for words has, alas, become estranged to...her."

"Children?"

"We tried."

"I'm sorry."

"I am not. Alonzo, unfortunately, would not make a good father. Diana wanted children, but there are problems, as they say, with the plumbing."

"Oh."

"And Ivy? Does Ivy want children?"

"Not yet. Someday, maybe."

"With Edmond?"

"Maybe."

"With other men?"

"I don't know."

"So," Crews said, "it's time for Alonzo to make the suggestion that we go somewhere and have illicit sordid sex."

"I was wondering when you'd get to that."

"So was I."

"Where would we go?"

"There are hotels with rooms."

"What would your wife say? Think?"

"Diana and Alonzo have a certain understanding about these things."

"Ivy was wondering when Alonzo would suggest such a *thing*," she said, trying to be funny, "and while it sounds interesting in that taboo-breaking sort of way, Ivy is going to have to say no."

This didn't phase Crews. "I understand. Never hurts to ask."

"Thanks for asking. I'm flattered."

"I could fall in love with you."

"I should probably head on home."

"To Edmond."

"Yes."

"Make love to him tonight, for me."

Ivy said, "I will."

Outside, Crews said, "There's someone I know, a former student actually; she's an editor now and she's looking for an assistant. I'll give her a call; then *you* call her. Forget proofreading."

"Thank you, Alonzo."

He kissed her on the forehead and wandered off to the subway station, back to Brooklyn.

Ivy took a different subway.

Three days later, she interviewed with Sharon Taylor, a thirty-five-year-old editor at Walcott & Sheridan, Inc. The editor didn't need to find out much to know what Ivy wanted, where Ivy was going.

"Alonzo Crews gives you a glowing recommendation."

"He's kind."

"I'm going to ask a personal question, probably unprofessional, but here it goes. Are you sleeping with the old man?"

"No," Ivy said.

Sharon Taylor nodded. "Good. Don't get me wrong, I love the old man. I learned a lot from him. But sleeping with him - I was your age and somewhat the wide-eyed thing. Now I'm not such a fool. At least I hope not. Who knows? You know what? I'm going to offer you the job."

"Thank you."

"I'm a hard-ass. There will be long hours and the pay - the pay is what you expect in this business."

"Better than what I'm getting now."

"Are you ready?"

"I'm ready," Ivy said.

THE BEST GAME IN TOWN

After making pizzas, Edmond found a bartending job and while he was making more money with the tips, he wasn't all that happy. He felt - had been feeling - he should be doing something else. Something different. Something better. He was starting to wonder if he made a mistake following Ivy to New York. Was his mother right? She'd never let him forget.

"You see," she'd say, "I told you so!"

Then he met Mark Gerrick. Mark was a stockbroker and often went to the bar where Edmond worked, along with other young brokers out to relax, have a few drinks, unwind after a long day on the phones; the bar was one of those small basement joints in lower Manhattan - dark and musty and individual. Edmond usually went in around four, worked until midnight or one. Three days a week. Mark Gerrick and his co-workers were in their early to mid-twenties; they were bright, energetic, cocky and on the road to riches. Or so they said. Edmond didn't have any reason to doubt them, they seemed to be well-off, wearing $1,000 suits and tipping better than any other customer.

One night, as Edmond finished his shift, Gerrick and two of his cohorts were still there and drunk.

"Hey, man, hey, Eddy, join us."

"Well," Edmond said.

"Oh come on, join us, we like you."

Edmond didn't see the harm. He didn't drink on the job, but he was off the clock and he could use a beer.

"Don't you guys have to be up early?" he asked, sitting at their small round table. "Don't you sleep?"

"Sleep?" Gerrick laughed, and so did his friends. "Who the fuck needs sleep? *Fuck* sleep. We're Supermen, we don't sleep."

"Nothing a little nose candy can't help, when the time for help is needed," one of the others said.

"I like sleep," Edmond said.

"When we're middle-aged millionaires," Gerrick said, "we will sleep. We'll sleep in our Westchester homes, our yachts moored in Montauk. We'll sleep as our stash is making outrageous interest points in secret offshore accounts. For now, we're young and hungry and snooze time is the enemy."

"Here here," said the others.

"So you guys work on Wall Street," Edmond said.

"We're the fucking future of The Street, buddy."

This is what happened. Edmond drank and talked to these guys for a few hours. They seemed to like Edmond, and Mark Gerrick suggested that Edmond ditch his slave job and go for the bucks. The two were alone on the street, standing near the subway drop. "I'll put in a good word for you," Gerrick said, "and I have *an eye*, I can read people—I fucking better for what I do. You're raw, but you could be whipped into shape. You could be doing what I do, making the money. Hell, you might even be able to make more money than me."

"Oh come on," Edmond said. "I don't know anything about the stock market."

"Either do I. Hardly anyone on The Street does, except for those old fuckers who went to Harvard and think they know all shit. *They don't know fucking shit.* This is 1987, man; this is the brave new world! I'm a salesman, Eddy. I'm a damn good salesman. I could sell anything. I *do* sell anything. You sell booze. We're all salesmen, Eddy. It's how the fucking spinning globe works."

Edmond nodded. He was cold. He wanted to go home.

"Think about it. Come by the office. We're always looking for new guys. Listen, you don't have to be some MBA whiz-kid and you don't have to be from some prep school with a father in the biz. Look at me. I'm a guy from Hoboken. Now I live in Manhattan. I have a very nice apartment, Eddy. You should come see it sometime. You should come see me at the office. I'll put in a word. We're become millionaires together. Our children will grow up rich and we'll look back on this moment, here on the dirty curb, and laugh our rich asses off."

Edmond did think about this when he went home, when he got into bed, when he snuggled against Ivy's naked and warm body. He was still thinking about it when he woke up.

Ivy was getting ready for work.

"You came home late," she said.

He told her about Mark Gerrick and the suggestion of a career change.

"He was drunk," she said. "Did you think he was serious?"

"I don't know."

"Can you really see yourself as a stockbroker?"

"I don't know," he said. "Why not?"

She was amused. "Yeah, I'd love to see you in a suit. I've *never* seen you in a suit. Have you ever *worn* a suit before?"

"To court."

"Oh yeah," she said distastefully, "court."

"It sounds like something different."

"It's different all right."

The next time Gerrick came into the bar, Edmond asked, "Hey, did you mean what you said the other night?"

"What did I say? How did I open my big mouth and make a fool of myself?"

"About helping me get a job at..."

"Oh yeah," Gerrick said. "Sure I meant it. Did you think about it? Hey, everyone, how about Eddy here joining the firm and pitching the shit with us? Fuck *yeah*, I meant it. Come by the office."

He went there two days later. Berryman & Associates was a small stock trading firm with two suites on the fifty-third floor of the World Trade Center.[*] A very attractive blonde in a tight black skirt and with a UV-bed tan sat at a desk in front of the double doors with the name of the firm embossed on the wood in cheesy gold.

"I'm here to help," she said, "how can I help?"

"I have an appointment."

"Yes, I'm sure you do."

"Mark Gerrick sent me."

---

[*] Later, Gerrick would tell Edmond how Bradford Barryman obtained these choice offices. "Brad got the digs, five years rent free, in a poker game. He won the space and free rent. Can you believe that?"
"Must have been some high stakes," Edmond said.
Gerrick said, "Bradboy always plays it high risk."
Much later, of course, Edmond would wonder if the story was true; if it wasn't just another tall tale that Bradford Berryman told to secure the heroic wonders of a life riddled with falsehoods and misinterpretations.

"Yes, I'm sure he did. What's your name?"

"Ed Foster."

"I'm Grace. You're going to work here?"

"I hope so."

"It has to burn, you know."

"What does?"

"The desire for money," Grace said. "It has to burn so much in your blood and your brain that it'll drive you to do amazing things."

That's exactly what Bradford Berryman said in the interview - or the orientation. Edmond sat in a conference room with half a dozen other young men in suits, filled out some paperwork and listened to Berryman. Berryman was in his late thirties, wearing suspenders and a tie; his shirtsleeves were rolled up; he was an intense, energetic man with rugged skin, bulging eyes and graying hair. He looked like Al Pacino; in another life, Berryman could have made a living as an Al Pacino impersonator. Berryman even had a Bronx accent. It was very weird.

"I hope none of you jackasses are going to waste my time. I don't have time to waste. If you want to waste my time, leave. If you want to learn how to make money, then you've come to the right place. But you gotta *want* that money so bad that it hurts like a mofo. You," he pointed to the fellow sitting next to Edmond, "if you work here at my firm, how much money would you like to make the first year?"

"I don't know," the fellow said, "about fifty thousand."

"Fifty *grand?*"

"Sure."

"Fifty?"

"It's a nice sum."

"Get the fuck outta here, you dipshit mofo," and Berryman pointed to the door. "Do you hear me?! Get off your ass and leave!

Fifty K ain't shit! It's chump change. Why do I still see your face?!? Skiddaddle and go make fifty g's selling vacuum cleaners!!!"

The fellow left.

Berryman turned to Edmond. "How about you, Mister? How much do *you* want in your first year?"

"One point two million," Edmond said.

Berryman clapped his hands. *"That's* what I want to hear. Now, that's a decent sum of cash. You ain't gonna make it in your first year, but you could come close. All you need to do is know that you deserve that money and it's out there and you can get it! You can get it here, and all you need is a bunch of telephone numbers and a goddamn fucking phone line! If everyone knew this, we'd all be fucked; but your average fuck out there doesn't know, your joe shmoe works his ass off making nothing. You gotta know how to play the game," and he stood up, raising his fists to the sky, "and by God this is the best game in town!"

That was it. Edmond and the others were told they'd get a phone call in two or three days if Berryman was going to offer a position. That night, at the bar, Mark told Edmond not to wait for that call. "You ring *him*, first thing in the morning."

THE NUMBERS GAME

Ivy helped him pick out three suits; she was excited to see her boyfriend in business attire. Edmond didn't like the tie and the starched shirt squeezing his neckline. He looked good in the mirror but felt gauche.

"You'll get used to it," Ivy said.

"Do I have to?"

"Yes, if you're serious about this career move."

"I'm serious," he said. "I think I am."

"You don't have to do this if you don't want to."

"We just bought these clothes!"

"Baby, we can take them back."

"I want to do this," he said.

"Give it your best shot. Why not? What do you have to lose?"

"The money on these suits."

"It's just money."

"I could always go back to bartending. Waitering."

"Just don't go back to making pizzas."

"We haven't had pizza in a long time."

"I may never eat another piece of pizza in my life."

So off to Berryman & Associates he went, as a trainee. There were rules and other things to learn; he would work the phones but make no actual sales for three months before taking the Series 7 exam to get his broker's license. He was not *expected* to sell, he was on the phone to learn how to use the phone; if, by some miraculous chance, he called a person who actually wanted to buy stock, he'd transfer it to his sponsor, Dave.

Edmond had hoped Mark would be his sponsor. The sponsor was basically his boss, trainer, tormentor and coach. Dave was younger than Edmond, taller and very blonde; he paid Edmond's meager monthly trainee's draw from his own pocket.

"When you begin to make commissions," Dave said, "you'll pay me back."

The stack of three-by-five cards with phone numbers and contact info were stale, old, deadbeat and misleading. There was no way in hell Edmond was going to find someone to listen to his pitch; most of the time people would hang up or yell at him.

"It's a numbers game," Dave said. "Ninety-nine percent of the time you'll meet rejection. You live for that one percent when a sale is made; you make your living off that one percent; we keep this firm going on that one percent. You can't let it get to you; you can't let it turn your mind into gooey shit. You dial and dial and talk and talk. The hours will be long and you won't see much of your old lady. But let me tell you, when you get that first commission check, and that check is twenty, thirty, forty grand, the pain all goes away. You want to know what I made last month? Seventy-eight thousand dollars. Month before that, sixty-two. Before that, seventy-one. You don't believe me? I'll show you my fucking pay stubs. There are guys in here that pull paychecks in excess of a hundred grand. There are *millionaires* in this room with you. Think about that."

There was no sitting down on this job; you worked the phones standing up, walking around. Nearly a hundred men in the giant bull pen, computers everywhere, ticker signs running, mouths moving like little machines. Edmond had never been in a place with such concentrated energy. Everyone fed off each other, fueling one another, keeping the enthusiasm up. Bradford would walk in every half hour, look around, and find something wrong. "What the fuck you doing?!? Why aren't you selling?!? This is America, where we make money! Only in America do we create money out of thin air; everyone else in the world slaves for it!" Bradford would also give pep talks about certain junk bonds. He paid incentive bonuses to his top sellers in cold hard cash.

"Here," he'd go, "have ten grand in new one hundred dollar bills. Go buy yourself a really expensive bottle of champagne. Go buy your bitch something real nice."

All day, the men around him talked about the money they made; and they all loved to spend it. Every Friday, someone's name was drawn from a hat and that broker would pay for dinner and drinks. Mark encouraged Edmond to join the Friday night gang, make friends, learn the moves. Edmond was treated to very pricey booze and $50 steaks. He watched the wait staff get two thousand dollar tips. The brokers pissed their money away like forgotten dreams, knowing that tomorrow they'd earn it all back.

And Edmond would walk or take the subway home - beat, confused and destitute. He would come home late and Ivy would be asleep; he'd climb into bed next to her and say, "I don't think I know what money is."

He brought Ivy to a Friday night gathering once. Everyone was told to bring along the wife or mistress or significant other. "It's bitch night, boys!" Ivy was a hit, wearing a light blue mini dress and high heels, her hair spiked out in every direction. Mark was particularly enamored with her; he kissed her hand when she arrived and when she left. At work, Mark said, "Eddy, your chick is hot."

"Thanks."

"Where did you find her?"

"In my Christmas stocking."

"She got a sister?"

"She has a brother, if you're interested."

"Hey, fucker, you know I don't swing that way. You don't swing that way, do you?"

Every day, Mark would ask about Ivy; little things, like what she wore that day, what she watched on TV, what she had for dinner. Mark said something about how great her body must look naked, and Edmond said, "I have pictures. She looks marvelous, let me tell you."

"Pictures? *Nude* pictures?"

"Um."

"No shit?"

"Yeah."

"I don't believe you."

Edmond brought the pictures to work; he only showed them to Mark. Some were in color, some black-and-white. Mark rolled his eyes and whistled. He asked, "You take these?"

"Yeah."

"You're good with the camera."

"I goof around."

"You got a dark room?"

"Had a make-shift one in San Diego but not here."

"These are very nice, Eddy. Can I keep one?"

"Oh, I don't know."

"C'mon."

"I don't think I should."

"Why?"

"Ivy."

"She'll never know," Mark said, "if you don't tell her." Edmond was still hesitant. "Two hundred bucks," Mark said and took out his wallet, a wallet stuffed with cash.

"Two hundred?" said Edmond. "For a picture?"

"Make it five for two."

Edmond couldn't pass on five hundred dollars. Mark chose two Ivy pics in the raw and gave Edmond ten fifties, crisp and wrinkled bills alike.

"This is the first time I've been paid for my photographs," Edmond said. He felt like a pimp.

"Hey, now you're a pro," Mark said.

IVY & MARK

Ivy was used to the attention and suggestions of men; she knew how to keep them at bay and she knew all the little tricks they liked to play. She didn't know why she didn't see it coming with Mark Gerrick; maybe she was too preoccupied with matters at work; maybe she didn't anticipate the gall. Mark was a cocky guy. One evening Edmond and Mark came by the apartment and talked her into going to a bar for a drink. It was more like five or six drinks. Mark was very flirtatious and even made a comment about her "nice round ass." Edmond didn't seem to mind and they were all laughing: just friends out having a good time. Ivy, of course, had no idea that Mark possessed two nude photos of her. (Edmond had no idea that Mark had the photos taped to the wall by his bed and he would often masturbate looking at them.)

She didn't think it was weird when Mark called her at work and asked if he could buy her lunch. "Don't say no," he said, "I happen to be in the neighborhood and I'm starving and who the hell wants to eat alone?"

She was hungry, had skipped breakfast; she thought Mark was being nice, maybe he wanted to talk about Edmond and his future as a stockbroker. What she really wanted was the grilled chicken club sandwich at the deli two blocks down. She told Mark to meet her there in ten minutes. He had two beers on a table when she arrived.

"I can't drink during the day," she said.

"Just one."

"Beer is too heavy."

"Wine?"

"I'll have a Diet Pepsi."

"Two beers for me then," he said, smiling, guzzling the first one down. He didn't waste time telling her what was on his mind once their food was served. "You're in my head day and night," he told her, "and I think it will, soon, drive me crazy."

With a mouthful of food, Ivy looked at him curiously and said, "What?"

He reached out to take her hand. "You're the woman of my dreams. How much more blunt can I be?"

"Mark," she said, "I live with Ed."

"So," he said.

"So?" she said.

"There's chemistry between us," he said, "you can't deny that."

"What makes you think this is true?"

"I've *felt* it."

"I'm sorry," she said very seriously, "but it's not there."

She started to think about his kissing her hand the first time they met, his impudent behavior when they went to the bar. Had she given him false signals? Had she said something that he took to be more than it was?

"That's not true," Mark said, looking at his food. He glanced up and said, "I feel it, between us."

"I need to get back to work, Mark."

"No. Wait. Sit. *Please* sit. Finish your food."

"Thanks for lunch, but…"

"Don't go. Hear me out."

She sighed.

"You look so beautiful," he said, "in this light."

She stared at her food.

"I want to make love to you."

"I have to go."

"Why do you want to run away?"

"I want to get back to the office."

"You're in denial. You want to run away from your true life. You know you have feelings for me."

"Mark," she said, "I don't even *know* you."

"Then *get* to know me. I'll make a bold and brash suggestion here. We go to a hotel suite. I'll get the best suite in town. All I want is one hour. One hour to fuck you; to make love to you. Once we have sex, you'll know. You'll know who you belong with. You'll know what your life should be, what destiny means."

"Do you have any idea what you sound like?" she asked him, very seriously.

"Tell me, sweetheart."

"A madman."

"A man in love."

"Have you forgotten about Edmond? Your friend?"

"He's not my friend. We work together. He's a guy I know. I know a lot of guys."

"And do you hit on their girlfriends? Their wives?"

"They hit on me."

"You know what," she said, standing, "you make me sick. I took two bites out of that sandwich and already I want to puke."

"Sit down."

"I'll stand, thank you. I'll walk away, thank you." She started to go, then turned. "And what if I tell Edmond about this?"

"Tell him, and I'll make sure he's fired. He can go back to bartending."

"You're a real jerk."

"Oh, c'mon. I was joking. There's no need to tell Eddy. We can go to that hotel and fuck and you don't need to tell him. Do you think he tells you everything?"

"You gave it your best shot. You made the proposition, and I'm turning it down. Let's leave it at that, okay?"

Mark thought about it for a moment, and then said, "Okay. Shake hands on it? No hard feelings?"

She shook his hand. He moved to kiss the back of her hand. "Your skin smells like heaven," he said.

She didn't tell Edmond about the incident, didn't see the point. No harm was caused and Edmond thought the guy was his pal.

That Friday night, Mark showed up at the door of her apartment, knocking loudly. Ivy looked in the peephole. She didn't like seeing Mark. Edmond was on the Friday night thing with the boys from work.

"Go away," she whispered.

"Ivy?" he said into the door.

"Yes?"

"Open up."

"What is it? Why are you here?"

"I'm here because Eddy told me to come over. Isn't he there?"

"No."

"He said he would be."

She opened the door, leaving the hook-latch on. She could smell booze on Mark. He smiled and said, "Hi, pretty girl."

"My boyfriend," she told him, "is not home, and he didn't call to say he was coming home or that he invited company."

"I hope nothing happened to him."

"I'm sure he's okay."

"Can I come in?"

"I don't think that would be a good idea."

"We can wait for him."

"You know what," she said slowly, "I don't believe you."

"Are you implying that you don't trust me?"

"I'm saying that you should go."

"This isn't going so swell, this thing between you and me."

"There is no thing," she said sternly. "There is no you and me."

"There will be, you know. It's manifest inevitability."

She closed the door and locked it. He kicked the door.

"Let me in you goddamn stuck-up bitch!"

"If you don't go away right now, I'm going to call the police."

She could hear his breathing as he thought about this. He said, "You wouldn't do that."

"Yes I would."

"I'm not a monster."

"You're acting like one."

"I'm sorry," he said. "Ivy, I really am sorry. I don't know what the hell is wrong with me."

"Go home."

"Can I use your bathroom?"

"No."

"I really need to pee."

"There's an alley in back."

"I can't stop thinking about you."

"Three seconds, or I call the cops and you can pee in jail."

She heard him walk away. She was scared. She expected him to come back any minute, maybe smash the door in. She looked out the window and saw Mark walk down the street. She felt bad. What had she done to bring this on? How was she going to tell Edmond about it? She had to let him know; but when her boyfriend came home she again chose to keep the matter to herself.

Mark started to send her flowers at work; they came every day. They were elaborate assortments that cost a lot of money. The first one had a small card that apologized for his actions. Then the notes started to tell her things about predestination, true love and economics.

With me, one note said, *you'll be rich. Eddy will never be rich.*

Ivy's co-workers started to think her boyfriend was rich. Some of the floral arrangements were in the $200-300 range. "That live-in of yours starting to make money on Wall Street?" they asked. She smiled and shrugged; she didn't want anyone to know she had an obsessive admirer. Or was he a stalker? She hoped it would stop, but after two weeks the flowers kept coming so she started sending them back with the delivery driver.

"What should do with them?" the driver asked.

"Donate them to the hospital," Ivy said. "I don't want you to bring these to me again. I won't take them."

"I have to deliver them, lady. It's what I do. It's my job."

"Give them to your wife."

"I don't have a wife."

"Girlfriend."

"I'm a fag, lady."

"Then give them to," and she sighed. "Toss them in the trash."

"What am I supposed to tell my boss?"

She called the boss and explained the situation.

"They're bought and paid for," the floral store boss said. "Good money is being spent here."

"Listen," Ivy said, "do not, I repeat do *not* accept this guy's order."

"Not take his money? I can't do that."

"Do *not*, I repeat do *not* deliver the order."

"What should I tell him?"

"Tell him to get a fucking life," Ivy said.

Mark had the flowers re-delivered to the apartment. Edmond was there the day a thousand dollars worth of backlogged undelivered roses, daises and tulips showed up, along with Mark's many notes.

To this, all Edmond could say was: "What the hell?"

"I have something to tell you," Ivy said, and she told him everything. Edmond was stunned, but he wasn't surprised. He knew Mark was attracted to Ivy, but so were other men. They didn't do crazy shit.

"I wish you had told me earlier," he said.

"Well, *I didn't*. That doesn't matter. What matters is right now."

"I have to talk to him."

"And tell him what?"

"I have to let him know he's making a fool of himself."

"Maybe you shouldn't."

"It'll be okay."

"Are you mad?"

He smiled. "It's not like I'm going to get into a fist-fight with him. I'll tell him what's what, that's all. I'll tell him to lay off."

Ivy was skeptical and paced about the apartment when Edmond called Mark at home. He wasn't there. He tried Mark's line at the office.

"Good, he's not around," Ivy said. "Let's get rid of this junk," nodding at all the flowers, "and forget it."

"I think I know where he is."

"No you don't."

"I'll go check, and if he's not there—"

"You'll come right home?"

"Yes."

"You promise?"

"Yes."

A Sock in the Nose

He went down to the basement bar where he had recently worked. Mark was there with a couple of guys from the firm. He smiled and said hello to all, ordered a Tom Collins, and asked Mark if they could speak in private. Mark acted like nothing was wrong; the two sat in a booth and Mark said, "Do you like money, Eddy?"

"Listen."

"*You* listen. Answer me: do you *like* money?"

"Who doesn't?"

"Do you love it?"

"Who doesn't," Edmond said cautiously.

"If you want to be rich someday," Mark said, "don't do or say anything you'll come to regret. Don't piss the wrong people off, and don't make waves. You know what I mean?"

"Thanks for all the flowers, Mark. I had no idea you felt that way about me."

"Who knew I was a queer. You know about queers, don't you? Brad hates them. Won't have them around. Guys who get caught being queer, faggots who slip by and get hired - they immediately get fired."

"I'm afraid I must inform you that I'm taken," said Edmond. "I'm in a committed, loving relationship. I appreciate the interest, but I'm devoted. My heart belongs to her and only her. One day, we'll get married."

"Did you propose?"

"We've talked about it, when our careers are settled."

"You're a lucky man, then."

"I think I am. Maybe I haven't been realizing it lately, but I am. I'm not alone."

"Being alone sucks," Mark said in a tough voice.

"You won't always be alone."

"I'm sorry for what I have done. I feel terrible. It's not right."

"Forget it, okay?"

"We're cool?"

"We're very cool."

"Shake on it?"

Edmond shook Mark's hand. Mark yanked him forward, and with his other hand made a fist and punched Edmond in the nose. Edmond was in pain. He covered his nose, which was bleeding and swelling up.

Mark stood and yelled, "FUCK YOU! YOU HOMO!"

He stomped out of the bar. The bar was very quiet with surprise and amusement. The guys from the firm were wondering what the hell that was all about. What had he said to Mark? What had he done? The bartender on duty gave Edmond a towel for the blood, ice for the swelling. The guys from the firm were very curious. Edmond said it was nothing.

He found Mark in the hallway at his building, leaning against his apartment door and pleading for Ivy to come out and run away with him.

"Mark Gerrick."

Mark slowly turned toward Edmond.

"Get the fuck away from my door."

"I'll have her. She'll be mine," Mark said in a low voice. "I have to take her from you, Eddy. You don't deserve. *Listen*! You're *not* going to marry her; you're *not* going to make babies with…"

"Are you crazy?" Edmond said. "What the hell is the matter with you?"

"I'm a man who knows what he wants. Always been that way. I see something I want, I go and get it. I know what's meant to be, I don't hesitate to help God do his bidding. That's the difference between you and me, Eddy. I know my place in this world and you're still stumbling around with your head up your ass."

Two NYPD officers showed up then; they said they'd received a call and what was the problem here?

"There's no problems, officers," Mark said, straightening his tie. "I was on my way home."

"Hold on," an officer said. "Is everything all right?"

"No," Mark said, "but it's not a problem."

"There's been a misunderstanding," Edmond said, "everything is okay. Thank you for coming by."

"Who lives here?"

"I do."

"I'm on my way home," Mark said.

An officer looked at Edmond's face and said, "Your nose is bleeding."

"Shit," Edmond said, touching his face.

"Somebody hit you?"

"Door in a bathroom stall," Edmond said sheepishly.

Ivy came out into the hallway and said, "Officers, I called. I'm sorry but I made a mistake. It was a silly case of mistaken identity. This is my boyfriend and this here is our good and decent friend who's on his way home to feed his dog."

"Yes, my dog," Mark said.

"Look, do you think we like wasting our time?" an officer said. "What's the story here?"

"There is no story," said Ivy.

"Don't call 911 unless you really need to," an officer said.

Mark left. The cops waited for Edmond and Ivy to go inside.

"Should I have told them the truth?" she asked.

"I don't know. Would they care?"

"I was thinking it'd cause more trouble than good. You have to work with him."

"Work," Edmond said.

"Your nose. Did he hit you?"

"Yeah."

"Did you hit him back?"

"No."

"Good."

"I *wanted* to hit him," Edmond said. He wanted to inflict a great deal of pain on Mark.

"Maybe this will be the end of it," she said, but it wasn't.

THE SET-UP

When Edmond went to work the next morning, Grace stood up from her desk and held up her hand, shaking her head and biting her lower lip nervously.

"Mr. Foster," she said, "you can't go in."

"Why not?"

"You can't."

"What are you saying, Grace?"

She pressed something on her desk. The panic button, he thought.

"Grace," he said, "I have to get on the phones."

"I'm sorry," she said.

"Talk to me." He knew what was happening. Perhaps he should've turned and left. He wanted to see it for himself; wanted to know how far Mark went.

"Grace?" he said.

She was very uncomfortable.

"All I know is...you can't go in."

Bradford came out from the large doors, and he looked pissed. "Well, there he *is*. There *he* is. There he *mother*fucking is." Bradford took a deep breath and glared. "Why don't you turn your homo ass around, get on that elevator, and never set foot on my floor again, eh?"

"I don't understand," Edmond said.

"Yes, you do."

"Mark—"

Bradford led him toward the elevator.

"I didn't know you were gay, Eddy. I have a sort of unwritten policy. Call me a homophobe, sue me for discrimination, but the men who work under me eat pussy, you know what I mean?"

"I don't know what you mean."

"You made a pass on the wrong guy! How foolish is that?"

"I don't know what you heard…"

"Oh I heard plenty, cocksucker," Bradford said. "I see you got socked in the nose."

"Mark."

"Said you offered to suck his dick in the men's bathroom. So he did what any straight guy would do. He socked you one. I would've done more. I would've broken bones."

"That story is bullshit."

"Bullshit you say?"

"You believe Mark?"

"There were witnesses!"

"I have a girlfriend," Edmond said, "and Mark has been harassing her. He's been sending…"

"Girlfriend, *right.*"

"I'm fired?"

"Yep. There's the elevator. Have a good day, fruitcake. Oh," Bradford reached into his pocket, handed Edmond a business card. "My lawyer. You want to sue me, go ahead. Have your lawyer contact my lawyer and we'll play around in court for a decade."

Edmond left the World Trade Center.

A year and a half later, Bradford Berryman would be indicted by the Securities Exchange Commission and the Department of Justice, along with a lot of other fellows like Barry Minkow during the collapse of the whole junk bond fiasco.

THE NIGHT A VERY BAD THING HAPPENED

Ten months later, a very bad thing happened to Ivy. She had gone to a cocktail party with her boss, Sarah Taylor; it was a small gathering for the publication of a book of short stories by Paul Miner. Miner was one of Sarah Taylor's pet authors; his first novel had received some favorable attention and his stories were about the street bums, drug dealers, losers and prostitutes. No one at the party was really there to congratulate Miner or celebrate another book being thrown into the world; Ivy learned that these get-togethers were to gossip so you could say at another party, e.g., "You won't *believe* what an ass Miner made of himself and his new book - which isn't all that good."

Ivy thought Miner was a great writer, although socially awkward like most; he was six-foot-three with very thick glasses and a wandering eye. He liked to wear army fatigues, a long leather jacket, and a baseball cap. He appeared uneasy in this posh literary setting; he seemed like he'd be more comfortable hanging out in the Bowery or Hell's Kitchen with heroin addicts and teenage runaways. She was amused at Miner's attempt to flirt with her - he was sincere like a little boy. His innocence surprised Ivy who was familiar with the sex in his work. She was talking with

Miner and out of the blue, there was Alonzo Crews. Crews wore his trademark orange jumpsuit.

"Are you a slut?" Crews asked her.

The question caught her off guard. "What?"

Miner adjusted his glasses.

"The way you're holding that beer bottle, by the neck," Crews said.

She looked at the bottle of St. Pauli Girl.

"Only sluts hold them that way," Crews said and smiled. "So, again, are you a slut?"

"You're putting me on, Alonzo."

"I'm simply a curious man."

She wanted to kick him in the nuts.

Sarah Taylor walked over and said, "Alonzo, are you making trouble again?"

"Who? Me?" said Crews with a wide grin.

"He's being an ass," Ivy said, dangling the beer bottle by the neck.

"Come," and Sarah took Alonzo by the arm, "there's someone I want you to meet."

Ivy shook her head and drank her beer.

"Do you know Alonzo?" Miner asked her.

"Yes. You?"

"He's published a few of my pieces in *The Peach*."

"Of course."

"He means nothing by what he said."

"I know."

"The St. Pauli Girl," Miner said, pointing to the image on the label. "That's not just a barmaid with four mugs of beer. Her sultry outfit with the cleavage indicates she's a prostitute."

"What are you saying? She's both a waitress and a whore?"

"Exactly."

They both laughed.

She went home at eight. Edmond was at work, bartending again, this time in Brooklyn. At her door, someone grabbed her from behind. A hand covered her mouth, she was pushed inside. She was thrown to the floor, on her back; the intruder was on top of her. He had a hand under her skirt. He ripped her stockings, ripped her underwear; he was angry and determined.

"I'm going to fuck your brains out now, bitch."

It was Mark Gerrick. She tried to push him off. She tried to scratch him but he slapped her hand away, then he slapped her twice across the face. She tasted blood. "You want me to knock your teeth out? You want me to *hurt* you?"

"Don't," was all she could say.

"I've been waiting for this a long time."

Ivy found herself standing by the couch. She was looking down at her body; she was watching Mark fuck her. Why wasn't her body fighting him off?

He stood up and zipped his pants and ran a hand through his hair. "I know you liked it. You were wet. It was good. It was just like I pictured it. Did you come, baby?"

"Please go away."

"I might want seconds."

"Edmond will be home soon."

"No he won't. And so what? What will he do? I'll break his nose again." Mark knelt down and touched her face, her hair. Ivy looked at the ceiling. "If you call the cops, if you report me, it'll be worse. First, I'll deny it. I'll say you invited me over and seduced me. Then I'll take a baseball bat to your boyfriend's knees and make him a cripple. Then I'll hire a gang of bikers to snatch you up and make you pull a train with them all weekend. I bet you'd like *that*, huh? I'd like to watch that. How sexy would *that* be?"

She couldn't speak.

"I'll be going now. Think about what I said. Maybe we can do this again, Ivy Gaylord. Maybe we still have a future. Think about it, okay? I'll be going now, sweetheart."

She heard the door close. She remained on the floor for what seemed like hours. It wasn't even ten o'clock. She could feel her legs and arms; she could move. She drew a bath and sat in the water until midnight when the water was very cold. She checked her face in the mirror; the cut on the edge of her lip was minor. Edmond would probably never notice.

Edmond came home after two. She listened to him move about the apartment: getting food from the fridge, going to bathroom, undressing and sliding into bed like a long lost husband returned from the war.

"Hey," she said.

"You're awake."

"I've been...thinking."

He snuggled against her. "About?"

She couldn't tell him.

He kissed her neck and that made her feel cold.

"We should move," she said. "Get a better, bigger apartment. I think it's time. We have enough money saved."

"Sounds good to me."

"Let's start looking tomorrow. I want to be in a new place by next week."

"You're in a hurry."

"I could use a change," she said. "I hate this hole in the wall."

"Maybe I could set up a dark room, start taking photography seriously."

He tried making love to her but she said she needed to sleep, she said not right now. She didn't sleep, listening to Edmond's heavy breathing and occasional snores. In the morning, she got dressed and went to work and forgot about the bad thing that happened to her last night.

THE DEAL WITH PAUL MINER

He was born in 1955 on the island of Okinawa; his father was career military. He grew up in Texas because his father was transferred there. He was the middle child of two, had an older and younger sister. The older sister ran away or was abducted (he was never quite sure what was the real story) when she was fourteen. His younger sister died in car crash when she was ten; her mother, the driver, also died. Paul Miner felt he should have departed the earth with them, because he, too, was in the car; he was thirteen and survived and for the rest of his life he'd ask the cosmos: Why did I get left behind? The accident resulted in two broken legs, a few cracked ribs, a lot of cuts and bruises on his body, and the loss of his left eye. He wore a glass eye and the vision in his right was poor so he wore glasses. His father put on the tough act, saying things like "we must march on" and "it's just you and me against the odds, kid. It's time for us to be strong soldiers." At night, Paul would listen, from his bedroom, to his drunk father talking to his mother's ghost; his father would weep. During Paul's freshman second semester in college (San Francisco State University) two men in army uniforms paid him a visit. His father had committed suicide.

Paul asked, "What kind of gun?"

He was told, "A .38."

There was some money and property left in a will, along with documents concerning his older sister, Irene; official police reports and some from a private investigator in San Antonio. The leads indicated that Irene had set her sights on Hollywood to become a star. He remembered that Irene loved the movies and used to say, "Some day I'll be on the screen and you'll eyeball me and you'll say, '*Wow!* That is my big sister!'" According to the reports, the only acting jobs she'd managed were 8 mm loop stag flicks; she surfaced now and then as a stripper or a streetwalker.

Paul quit college. The money his father left could last five years, ten if he was frugal. Paul wanted to spend it. He went to Los Angeles in search of his sister. He was eighteen, so she'd be twenty-two. All he had were pictures of her at fourteen and thirteen; he was thinking maybe she hadn't changed all that much. He checked into a motel in the Fairfax district and hit the streets, showing his sister's photos to every hooker and pusher around. No one could help him. Many didn't trust him. Others thought he was on LSD. The hooker's would sometimes ask: "You wanna date?" One night, he returned to his room with a girl who had platinum blonde hair, long white legs and a very ample bosom. He paid her $20 to take his virginity. Over the next three months, he had sex with many prostitutes, almost a different one each night, their ages ranging from twelve to fifty. They all had unique and sad stories and he would pay to hear these tales; when they left, he'd scribble down their histories into notebooks which he labeled 'Case Studies of Whores.' A few of them resembled his sister, or what he thought his sister might look like now. He had a perverse fascination with the idea that he may have paid his own sister for sex and she didn't even know.

One whore told him, "I don't think your sister would still be on the streets after all these years."

"Why?"

"It's not something you do for a very long time."

"What do you think happened to her?"

"Honey, anything could have happened to her. She could have been murdered. You know how many of us get murdered every year? You don't read *that* in the papers. She could have gone straight. She *could* have gone with an agency, the high-class stuff. She could have found herself a husband, got her act together, and now has a house and some kids. Bottom line, she ain't out here, baby boy."

Paul did notice the constant turnover of prostitutes. For those who stopped and did something else, every day the buses and trains brought in fresh new bodies. Paul had to leave L.A. His task, he now understood, was futile; and his inheritance was quickly disappearing from paying out to the daily hookers.

He went to Las Vegas and lost more of the money to the black jack tables and expensive call girls.

One night he ordered a redhead to his hotel room at the Stardust. "She has to be a *true* redhead," he told the escort service. "The curtains have to match the carpet."

"We can do that, sir," a woman's voice said on the phone.

"She has to be young, eighteen to twenty-five, slender with a round face and a very kinky mind."

"We can do that."

He wasn't disappointed in the woman. She looked at the two bottles of champagne and asked, "What's the occasion?"

"You only live once."

"Yeah? I can dig that."

"Or twice," he said, "if you happen to be James Bond."

"What?"

"Forget it. Look. I want a *special* evening, just you and me."

"I specialize in special, big boy."

"Do you do golden showers?"

"I do anything."

"Golden showers and champagne it is!" Paul said.

"Are we celebrating something?"

"Yes we are. We're celebrating the fact that I'm almost broke; that I have blown my father's inheritance."

"And this is a happy occasion?"

"It means I'm free," he said.

He wasn't *that* broke, but close to it. He went to New York from there, renting a room in the Chelsea Hotel (based strictly on the literary connections), purchasing a typewriter from a pawn shop and an acoustic guitar from the music store near the hotel. He didn't know how to play the guitar. On the typewriter, he began writing two books: one transcribing his case studies on L.A. whores and another - a detective novel about a teenage girl who runs away from home. All the things that he imagined happened to his sister went into the book. When the books were done, he made photocopies and dropped them off at various publishers in the city. He never heard a word back. He tried to learn the guitar but could never get his big fingers to bend right. He discovered the whores living in the Chelsea so sometimes he'd pay them to stay the night in his bed. There were also other 'undiscovered' writers, actors, musicians and everything else inside the Chelsea walls; addicts, schizophrenics, and prophets - you name it. Paul felt at home; he was among people he understood, people who tolerated him.

He started to grow depressed. The publishers weren't offering him big bucks for his books. He would call the publishers and ask about his books; he'd be told they never received a submission from him, they had no idea who he was, he should get an agent, he should stop calling every other day, thank you, goodbye.

Heroin helped the pain. He never shot the stuff into his arm; he either snorted or smoked. His mind would take him back to Texas.

A year later he had no money left. He was kicked out of the hotel and living on the streets. Aside from the cold, the rain and the snow, being homeless wasn't too bad. There were many men and women like him; he could sit and talk with them for hours. Paul learned how to survive: how to find food in garbage cans, how to panhandle coins, how to steal purses from unsuspecting women.

Paul Miner woke up at 4:30 a.m. in the 14th Street subway station on March 17, 1982 and said to himself: "This is *not* a life." He went to the Salvation Army for help; he convinced the Christian soldiers that he was dead serious about becoming a productive member of society again. They gave him shelter, food, new clothes and two weeks to find a job. He was employed within twenty-four hours: the maintenance graveyard shift at a large printing press on Staten Island. He walked in and said, "I need work or else I'll die." He swept the floors, cleaned the bathrooms, washed the windows, and listened all night to the machines churn out newspapers, brochures and catalogues.

He moved back into the Chelsea and it was like he'd never left. Wait. That's not true. He was older, he was focused; he vowed to never let himself go to hell again. He started publishing his stories in magazines both small and large. He wrote book reviews for academic journals. He started to write porn novels for a little company in Jersey City. Atlantic Editions always needed people to whip out 35,000-word manuscripts of smut and they paid $750 a pop. Paul could do this over the weekend, drop the product off to New Jersey and then head to work. The publisher of these throwaway paperbacks with X-rated covers would say, "What are you giving me here? There's some good stuff, this is almost like art. There's enough sex, but leave your art to art, leave your best to the real novels." Paul wrote a dozen of these books under two pen names: Paul Masters and Kimberly Hunt. One day the publisher called and said they were going to do a line of adult westerns— there would still be plenty of sex but with an emphasis on plot and violence (lots of shoot-outs with pistols and rifles). The pay was $1,000 per book, flat. He wrote three.

In 1985, at the age of thirty, Paul Miner finished a 990-page novel called *Now I Know What Happened to Me*. When asked what it was about, Paul would answer: "Alas, those who have no roof over their heads." He went to the publisher of Atlantic Editions and said,

"I need an agent. Do you know any agents you can introduce me to?"

"No, I'm afraid not."

"Not one?"

"Well, there is one. But you have to swear on your grave you didn't get her name from me. She'd sooner slit her throat than be associated with Atlantic Editions or me. She's a prominent literary agent. She happens to be my ex-wife, man, so my name never comes up. Say you saw her listed somewhere."

Paul walked his hefty manuscript to the mid-town suite of The Yolanda Wallenstein Agency and left it there with the office assistant, as Yolanda Wallenstein was at a conference in South Dakota.

The agent called two months later and said, "I think I can sell this. No promises, but I'll do my best and we can see what happens."

Paul was very excited but he wasn't going to show it. He said, "Okay, yes, that would be nice. Yes, please try to sell my book."

The book was rejected by half a dozen houses; those who read it said they liked it, they thought it was well-written, but in the end it was too depressing, too long, too wordy, too un-hip; they liked that Miner was thirty, he was young, young was "in," but everyone wanted the next *Less Than Zero* or *Bright Lights, Big City*. One editor suggested the book be changed into a thriller or horror, that a plot element cause the protagonist to rise up and be a hero. In most cases, Yolanda Wallenstein would give up on a property after three or four declines, but she believed in his novel. She had lunch with Sarah Taylor at Walcott & Sheridan and told Sarah about *Now I Know What Happened to Me*.

A week later, Yolanda phoned Paul and said, "I have someone who wants to buy your book."

Paul was very excited but he wasn't going to show it. He said, "Okay, yes, that would be nice."

"Two things before they'll make an offer. You have to cut it by a third and change the title to something catchy - commercial. *The Bum.*"

Paul sighed.

"It's business," the agent said.

Paul used the small advance for a vacation to Thailand where, for two weeks, he swam in a sea of pretty young brown-skinned prostitutes. At all times he had three in his bed, attending to various parts of his body. He wrote a long essay about the experience, selling the piece to a big men's magazine. The men's magazine paid him well and said they'd love more stories in the same vein. *The Bum* was published a year later and by that time he was getting so many magazine assignments he quit his night job and found a real apartment.

How Paul Learned Ivy's Darkest Secret

Sarah Taylor got a better job at another publishing house. Paul would have gone with her. Unfortunately, he was contracted to deliver two more books to Walcott & Sheridan over the next five years. Ivy was promoted to associate editor, inheriting a few of Sarah's authors.

Like Paul.

Paul had a 1440-page manuscript for her to tackle.

"All you need to know," he told her, "is that I don't see myself as a novelist or fiction writer. I'm a journalist. The books look like fiction but they're reporting, pure and simple. What I'm getting at is - I'll tell you this. My first book. *The Bum.* That wasn't the real title; I hope one day it can be reissued under its true title. And 300 pages were taken out. I couldn't say much because I was unknown and I needed to get that book published. I promised myself I would never let that happen again." Nevertheless, Ivy called him three days later and said the book was simply too long.

"It's not a feasible length," she said.

"Is that you or the sales people talking?"

"Me."

"I wouldn't know where to cut it. Everything is vital."

"I have some ideas. Hear me out, okay? Let's get some coffee and talk face to face."

Over coffee, Paul informed Ivy he thought she was very pretty 'as always.' She didn't pay attention; he spoke like a small mouse. Ivy was weary of most men now; she seldom tolerated innuendoes or suggestions and would verbally assault any man who tried. She spent half an hour going over the sections she felt could be taken out. Paul shook his head slowly the whole time.

"We would be here all night if I went over why it can't be done. To put it simply; the book would be ruined."

"Okay," Ivy said. "I talked to my boss and he's willing to offer a compromise: take a twenty percent cut in your advance and he'll give you 1200 pages."

Paul said sourly, "Lose twenty percent of my money and 240 pages of my book."

"You have to consider the economics. The cost of paper and shipping. What people are willing to pay for a book that size. It's going to be at least 900 pages in finished form."

"I'm not an unreasonable man."

"No, you're not. I know this."

"Will you and I be working closely on the edits?"

"Very."

She worked with Paul for two weeks, either at the office when she had an hour or the coffee shop. Little by little, whole pages and chapters were removed. There was one part where Paul was resistant; Ivy stated her case and said her position was firm.

"I'm willing to compromise," Paul said. "We can cut the part if you let me rub your toes and feet."

"What?"

"I think I've acquired a foot fetish."

She asked, "Why does every man in the city have to make sexual overtures to every woman he meets?"

"Because they're men," Paul replied.

Ivy would never know what motivated her to go to Paul Miner's apartment on East 52nd Street. Maybe because she felt completely safe. She took off her shoes and let Paul do what he wanted with her toes and her ankles and her heels. He caressed, he rubbed, he licked; he sucked. It felt very nice. Then she saw herself taking her clothes off and getting into his bed. Paul was naked. She wasn't attracted to the man but she was going to let him make love to her anyway.

No.

No, she couldn't.

She said, "No, I can't. I'm sorry."

She started to get dressed.

"I don't understand," Paul said, hurt. "Did I do something wrong?"

It all came out like an atomic bomb exploding near a dam. She began to cry. She sobbed. She wailed. She moaned. Paul held her to him and told her it was all right.

"It's not all right," she said. She needed to confess so she told him everything; how a man named Mark Gerrick raped her two years ago, how she pushed it deep inside her like it had never happened, how she never told her boyfriend, how she started to become distant, aloof; she was seldom intimate with her boyfriend anymore and when they were, it was like she wasn't there, she wasn't in her body; how in the past six months she let herself be picked up in a bar by a stranger, pretending she was someone else and trying to enjoy sex. She thought that coming here would be something like that. She said ever since her rape she hadn't shed a tear and it was good to finally let it out.

"I'm sorry that happened to you," Paul said, holding her face in his hands.

"I'm sorry for laying all the heavy shit on you."

She didn't know how Paul thrived on human drama like this.[*]

"Have you talked to any kind of—professional in these matters?" Paul asked. "There are people who can help. Doctors..."

"I haven't even admitted that it happened to me - until now. Like it was someone else's memory."

"Maybe you should tell your boyfriend."

"No. I can never do that."

"You need to tell someone."

"I've told you."

Paul smiled. "Indeed you have. Thank you for confiding in me. I feel useful now."

"I'm sorry I can't sleep with you. I hope you understand."

"I *do* understand."

"And I have to ask you to keep this between us. This is our secret. Please don't tell anyone about...what happened to me."

"Who will I tell? *Kirkus*?"

She laughed.

"Can I tell *you* a secret now? I've never had a girlfriend," Paul said matter-of-factly. "No one's ever loved me and while I have been infatuated with many women - and I'll admit I'm infatuated with you - I've never been in love, the reciprocated kind. Any and every woman I have been in bed with has been a

---

[*] "When inward life dries up," once wrote Rollo May in *Love & Will*, "when feeling decreases and apathy increases, when one cannot affect or even genuinely touch another person, violence flares up as a daimonic necessity for contact, a mad drive forcing touch in the most direct way possible."

prostitute. This is okay. It defines the roles; it forces things to be commercial: the buyer and the seller."

Ivy didn't know what to say. She could've told him that eventually he'd find someone. It sounded like bullshit.

"I should go home now," she said.

"Do me a favor. Make love to your boyfriend; make love to him like you did when you first met him. Be there. You need to do this for your health."

He was right. Edmond was in his darkroom when she arrived to the apartment on West End Avenue. She knocked on the darkroom door and said, "Hey! Hey you in there! Come out come out. I'm *horny!"*

Edmond was pleasantly surprised. His clothes smelled like chemicals so she took the clothes off him. Everything seemed perfect until the sex started to happen. Ivy jumped out of her body; she looked at herself with Edmond and thought: no.

WHAT WAS EDMOND DOING?

He was bartending at night, taking pictures during the day. He was actually a semi-professional photographer, which pleased him very much. He was getting assignments from two small newspapers, one in Brooklyn and one in Long Island - community papers trafficking in fluff stories; and occasional gigs from young, hip, start-up magazines that needed pictures of bands, artists and future multi-millionaire computer geeks. Edmond took several photos of Ivy on New Year's Eve 1989.

He said, "Hold up your champagne and smile." She smiled, but when Edmond would look at these pictures later (after he left Ivy for Natalie and Natalie gave him a baby) he'd think that she appeared very sad.

How Edmond and Paul
Identified with Each Other

Edmond took pictures of Paul Miner while he worked on the manuscript to a collection of essays called *Case Studies of Hookers, Whores, Prostitutes and Call Girls.* Ivy was in the pictures. The two tried to look hard at work but there was little work to do. The book was 245 pages, concise and polished. Paul came to Edmond and Ivy's apartment. A Japanese girl in her late teens with stiff pink hair from a magazine called *Mulching the Zeitgeist* came along to interview Paul. Ivy liked the magazine; she thought the readership ideal for Paul. She told the magazine she knew the *perfect* photographer and he worked for cheap! Paul told the girl from the magazine that he'd written the first draft of this new book not long after he became homeless.

"Wow," the girl said. "You were, like, homeless?"

"Wow," said Paul. "Yes, I was."

"What was *that* like?"

"It wasn't a picnic."

"How did you survive?"

"I still ask was myself that question."

"How long were you homeless?"

"Too long."

"That's when you hung out with prostitutes?"

"No, that was before. In L.A. In Vegas."

"You slept with them?"

"Oh yes."

"How did you pay for them?"

"I had money then."

"Wow."

"I know."

"We're all fans of your shit, you know. At the mag."

"I thank you all."

"We think you're *awe*some."

"I like your hair," Paul said. "You look like a character out of those cartoons. Anime."

"Yeah," she said, "that's the idea."

Paul and Edmond had met briefly before. Paul was interested in Edmond's photos so Edmond showed him what he had. Paul was impressed; he thought Edmond had an eye for catching that "something else." For instance, the photos of Ivy on New Year's Eve; Paul immediately spotted the disconsolation, that Edmond couldn't see; wouldn't see until later. So, the three went out for drinks. Paul knew Ivy hadn't told her boyfriend her secret, and he honored his promise. Paul knew it was *important* that he became a part of their lives for their sake, for his own work. He said he could probably get Edmond assigned to him for one of his newspaper pieces. Edmond's response: "You swing it, I'll do it."

Edmond first teamed up with Paul for a feature piece in a big liberal weekly paper; the topic was crack cocaine. Paul was fascinated with people who were hooked on crack, from the street whore in Alphabet City to the money manager on the Upper East Side. Paul and Edmond spent three days hanging out with crack heads, dealers and users alike, talking to them, photographing them, smoking with them. Everyone wanted their picture taken, everyone was a ham—except for one dealer who called himself Twenty ("I live for the twenty-dollar rock") who was afraid the cops might see his picture. There were some crimes, he explained, and he wasn't interested in going to jail just yet.

"I'm a smoker and a seller," he said, "and there's a lot of smoking and selling to do before my time's up in this worl'." Twenty was a tall man, over six-foot-six; his jeans were always dirty and his teeth were piss yellow. He was black. All the crack smokers seemed to be black; Paul and Edmond were usually the only white men the run-down, roach-infested, smelly motels and flops.

"*Suck* that pipe, baby," the crack whores would tell Paul, laughing and slapping their flabby naked legs, "suck it like a *dick,*" and Paul would puff on the dirty glass pipes. The whores were more than happy to share their pipes. Paul was buying "the rock" that would leave resin they could later scrape for a few tokes. The stuff was harsh but good. Edmond liked the way his mouth and throat would numb up, how his scalp would tingle, how he would feel invincible for three minutes; this sensation would go away so he had to take another hit off 'the glass penis.' Crack also made Edmond horny, but he wasn't about to go near the whores. Paul would give them some money for blowjobs or quick fucks. The whores would play with the hair on Edmond's head and go, "C'mon, baby, I know you feel like it, I'll even give you a free one. I'll make you feel so goooooood."

"He won't do it," Paul would say, "he's a married man."

"Really? You married?"

"I have a girlfriend," Edmond would say. "We've been together so long, it's like being married."

"She'll never know."

"Oh she might."

He wasn't tempted, even though his sex life with Ivy was practically non-existent. He hadn't really thought about this until now: here in some crappy room in the asshole of New York smoking crack with three whores while a fourth sucked on Paul's cock. He took some pictures. Paul smiled and waved to the camera.

The excursion ended when Twenty and some of his buddies surrounded Edmond and Paul and demanded money.

"You don't want to do this," Paul said.

"I *have* to do this, *white boy,*" Twenty said. "We *sick* of yo' asses. Whada fuck's up with you white boys? Gimme yo' cash."

"Look," Paul said.

"*You* look," said Twenty, "gimme yo' money or me and my homies here gonna *fuck* yo' shit up."

Paul sighed and gave Twenty what he had; about a hundred bucks.

"All I have is this," and Edmond handed over a five and two ones.

"Whadda fuck?" said Twenty. "Gimme the camera."

"You don't need a camera," Paul said.

"I can sell the shit," said Twenty.

"No," Edmond said.

"Let's fuck em up," one of Twenty's homies said.

Paul roared like a Viking, lunged after Twenty's crew. They all ran away except Twenty, saying: "Crazy white fucker!" Twenty tried to grab Edmond's camera and Paul punched him on the side of the head. Twenty pulled out a small knife and stabbed Paul in the gut. Paul punched Twenty in the face, breaking Twenty's nose. "I want my money back," Paul said. Twenty dropped the cash and muttered something about revenge, and walked away with a defiant bounce.

Paul touched his abdomen and said, "Ouch."

"You okay?"

"My jacket took most the blade. It's just a flesh wound."

Paul didn't want to go to the police or the hospital. They took a cab to Paul's apartment. The wound wasn't deep and had stopped bleeding. Paul applied a small towel and gauze to himself and told Edmond he wanted to get drunk. Edmond needed a drink; he was still shaking. Paul brought out a bottle of vodka and two glasses. The two sat and drank and talked about their lives. Paul explained what happened to his older sister, how he searched for her in Hollywood and became acquainted with the whores. He almost told Edmond about what happened to Ivy, the guy who raped her - it almost slipped out. He stopped himself. He couldn't do it. He would betray Ivy if he did. Ivy was violated and there was no justice. He decided he had to do something about the injustice.

"I should go home," Edmond said.

"You should," Paul said; "you have a very beautiful, very precious woman waiting for you at home."

LOOKING AT IVY SLEEPING

Edmond thought she was so goddamn beautiful in a painful way; asleep or awake, he always felt this for her and this made him very sad because something wasn't right between them.

In the morning, Ivy asked, "So what did you and Paul do last night?"

He said, "Nothing really."

Ivy said, "Why don't I believe that?"

DREAMING OF THAILAND

Paul had looked up where Mark lived back when Ivy had confessed her pain to him. *Just in case he does it again*, Paul had told himself. Mark was not home. Paul waited, leaning against a tree, staying in the shadows. At three a.m., a drunk man in a suit and overcoat stumbled down the street, walked up to the building. Paul was watching. Paul approached the man.

"Hey there, hello."

Mark turned. "Hello."

"Excuse me, but are you Mark?"

"Do I know you?"

Paul stood close. "Are you Mark Gerrick?"

Mark was drunk and was not afraid. "Yeah, I am."

"That's all I wanted to know," said Paul, "I didn't want to do what I am about to do to the wrong man."

"Do what, big guy?"

"This."

Paul head-butted Mark Gerrick. Mark fell back. Paul punched Mark in the face, and then the chest. Mark went down.

Paul threw Mark down the stairs and onto the pavement. He knelt down, his knee on Mark's Chest.

"This is for Ivy," Paul said. He proceeded to break several fingers on Mark's right hand, and then his left. He did this fast. Then he broke both of Mark's wrists. Mark screamed loudly.

"Let's see you make phone calls and sell junk bonds this way," Paul said. He grabbed Mark's head and smashed it on the sidewalk twice. Mark's eyed rolled into the back of his head and he was unconscious. Or dead. There was a lot of blood seeping out of his skull. People were looking out their windows. Paul got up and walked away, fast. He could hear sirens. Blood was on his hands. He kept them in his pockets and walked down the nearest subway entrance on the street.

In the morning, he flew to Thailand. Paul wanted to take Edmond to the special land 'where the girls are so young and pretty it's baby pussy heaven.' Paul had returned to Thailand many times since his first visit and his first book. Any time he could get a magazine or newspaper to foot the bill, he was on a jet. Ivy thought Edmond should go. "You should expand your horizons, see the world," she said, although she'd never been out of the country herself.

In Bangkok, Paul would take Edmond to all the bars where a man could find Thai whores. They would have fun. Edmond would learn that many of these girls usually didn't make it past the age of twenty; they were either murdered or contracted AIDS. The whores would be cheap and resplendent and they would be happy and ignorant and only want sex all the time. Edmond would wake up in the middle of a hot sticky night with two girls sleeping under each arm; he would still be high from whatever it was he'd been smoking - opium or a weird native plant that made him fuck like a bull. In the morning he would think it was all a dream because the girls were gone; then he'd discover the girls in the other room with Paul, one sucking Paul's cock and the other licking Paul's ass.

"You join us!" the girls would say. "Join us we have fun!"

Yes, that is what would have happened—and they would return to the United States, Edmond back to his beautiful, fragile woman and Paul back to his ugly, insipid loneliness.

But Edmond didn't go to Thailand; he didn't go anywhere.

Where He Was the Day it Happened

Martin Tucker was in a hotel room two blocks away and having sex with a married woman when the first jet hit the World Trade Center. He looked up and said, "What was that?"

The married woman, Sharon, said, "Tuck?"

Some people called him Tuck.

They both went to the window and looked. They were on the tenth floor of the downtown hotel with a good view of the World Trade Center.

"Something happened," Sharon said.

She wanted to continue fucking but he wasn't in the mood; when the second jet hit the WTC, he saw it. He was looking out the window and he saw it coming. Sharon was putting her black underwear back on. He witnessed the explosion and the fire. The hotel shook and Martin Tucker, who hadn't felt fear in a very long time (he hadn't even felt good in a long time) was terrified and worried and said, "Sharon, get your clothes on," and they got the hell out of the hotel. When they were finally on the street, the WTC came crashing down and people were screaming among the smoke and dust and debris and human bodies and the pieces of human flying in the air. Sharon let go of his hand and she ran; she ran away from him, probably back to her husband, Curtis.

Martin was alone.

Sharon had called his cell phone at eight a.m.

"I don't have anything on my calendar this morning," she said.

"I don't have to be in court until one," she said.

"Let's get a hotel room and fuck all morning," she said.

She was a lawyer, thirty-seven, married, having an affair. He was an editor, forty-one, divorced and he didn't have anything pressing to do besides a sales meeting at three.

He'd said, "Sure."

They'd gone to their favorite hotel downtown.

"You should just leave Curtis," Tucker had said when they were getting undressed.

"And do what?" Sharon had said. "Be with you?"

He'd shrugged.

"Somehow I don't think you're want to get back into a relationship," she said.

"You have a point."

"I like this arrangement."

"It's a pretty good arrangement."

He liked sneaking to hotel rooms in the morning and engaging in rough sex. That's what they were doing when the first jet slammed into the WTC.

So many people running and screaming reminded him of the Godzilla movies. He didn't realize he was covered in soot until he looked at his hand and saw the gray.

His cell phone rang.

"Daddy?" his ten-year-old daughter's voice said.

"Cassandra," he said.

"Daddy, what's going on?"

"Where are you?" he asked.

"School." She was on her Nokia. He'd bought it for her ninth birthday. "I'm leaving. I don't want to stay here. I'm going to get a taxi and go home."

"You do that," he said. "You go home."

"Will you come see me?"

"I will," he said. "I will immediately."

He didn't know what to do and he wasn't quite sure where he was going; so much confusion and madness - car alarms going off, dust-covered frightened people running. A man sat on a curb and spoke in a thick Long Island accent:

"Oh my God oh my God oh my God."

Tucker walked back to his office at the publishing company. His office was on the eighth floor. Radios were on; the news was coming in from all sources, even from Howard Stern. He thought that was funny.

No one said hello to him; no one knew he'd stepped out. He went into his office and sat down. He looked at his desk and thought: 'There's too much paper in the world.'

His assistant, Brenda Cavuto, walked in. Her mascara was smeared; the only times he ever saw her with smeared mascara was after he fucked her. He felt like crap. He knew he had no business going to bed with Brenda, a twenty-two-year-old woman with too many idealistic notions about the publishing industry. Many times he had hired young women fresh out of college, always knowing it was a bad idea because he was hiring them with the intent of fucking them. So he would fuck them, and the young women would go off and do something else; get married or an editorial job at another house.

Brenda said, "Tuck, where were you?"

"The world is going crazy," he said.

"I'm scared."

"I know."

"Are you scared?" she asked.

"I don't know what I am," he said.

"Will you hold me?" she said.

"Yes," he said, "I will."

She curled up in his lap. She was a heavy girl, or he was an old man who couldn't hold a girl like he used to. He grabbed her legs; she pressed her face into his neck and cried mascara on his skin.

It wasn't easy to get a cab. Martin finally managed to hail one to take him to his former home on West End Avenue. He looked up at the building that he used to call home. Pieter, the Russian doorman, was there. Pieter was crying.

"Mr. Tucker," Pieter said. "Mr. Tucker, you're not supposed to be here, are you?"

"How are you?" Martin asked. "What's wrong?"

"I was a soldier in Chechnya," Pieter said.

"Yes," Martin said.

"I came to America to get away from these kind of bad things," Pieter said. "And now the shit has followed me here!"

"Listen," Martin said, "I need to see my daughter. Cassandra. Casey, you know. I told her I would."

"She came home half an hour ago."

"I know I'm not supposed to be here, Pieter..."

The doorman nodded. "I understand. I understand very much."

Cassandra was shaking. "Oh Daddy," she went, and leapt into his arms, and buried her small face into his neck.

"Baby girl," he said, "little one - it's okay."

He looked around. There was no sign of Francesca. He asked, "Where's your mother?"

"I don't know."

Martin let Cassandra down, onto her feet. "You don't know?"

"I've been trying to call her cell phone. She's not answering."

Martin didn't know how he felt about this. Francesca wrote content for a big web site.

"Daddy?"

"I'm sure she's all right."

"Are *you* all right?"

He had to think about that.

"Yes," he said, "I believe I am."

They sat down in the living room and watched the news on TV. Every channel had coverage of the jets crashing into the WTC and the towers coming down. Cassandra held his hand, and every time she saw another shot of the plane smashing into a tower, she squeaked and tightened her grip.

Martin didn't know if it was a good idea, letting Cassandra watch the carnage. How could he keep it away from her? The whole world was watching, and his daughter had lived through the horror of his divorce.

"What the fuck, Tuck?"

Francesca had walked in, her hair sticking up, her eyes darting back and forth; she saw Martin and Cassandra sitting together, holding hands.

"Mommy!" Cassandra said, a scowl on her small face. "Don't be mean!"

"What are you *doing* here, Tuck?"

He said, "I'm glad you're alive and well, too, Fran."

"What are you doing here," Francesca said, stamping her foot, "what are you *doing* here, you're not supposed to be here, you're *not* supposed to even set foot in here unless it's visitation day, and it's *not* visitation day. This is against the *court order*, Tuck. What do I have to do? *What do I have to do?* Call the police?"

"I think the police are busy right now."

"What?"

"What? Don't you know what's going on?"

He pointed to the TV.

"Do I *know* what's going on?" Francesca said. "Look at me! Just look at me! Of course I know what's going on! What I want to *know* is what the hell gives *you* the idea that you can just *come* into *my* home! Like you still *live* here or something…"

Cassandra screamed, *"I asked him to come here!"*

"That's not *right*," Francesca said to her daughter, "you know that's not right! You had no business asking this *bastard* to come here at a horrible time like this! I have *friends* who work in those buildings!"

Cassandra screamed again ran to her mother and said, "You *bad* Mommy," and punched her mother in the stomach. The girl put her weight into the swing. Francesca gasped and stepped three steps back. She looked like she'd been stabbed.

Martin got between the two to avert any further violence.

"Enough," he said.

"Oh my God," Francesca said: very, very softly.

"I fucking hate you *both*," Cassandra said.

Martin Tucker left the building. He said goodbye to Pieter the doorman, but Pieter was staring at the wall, listening to the news on a small portable radio. The air was thick with godlessness.

He thought of Sharon. He hoped she was all right. He called her cell phone on his cell phone. It took five times; he kept hearing an electronic voice say: "We're sorry, but all circuits are busy."

Sharon answered on the third ring.

"It's me," he said.

"Hi," she said.

"Where are you?"

"Home."

"Are you—okay?"

"I'm in the bathroom." Her voice was low. "Curtis is here."

"How is he?"

"He *knows.*"

"What's that?"

"I said he knows. About us. He always did. Who did I think I was fooling?" she said.

"I'm the fool," she said.

"It's all so crazy," he said. "We saw it happen from the window."

"He said he still loved me."

"We had no idea..."

"Despite what I did to him, he still loves me. He says he understands. How can he understand?"

"A lot of people are dead."

"We can't see each other, not after this," Sharon said. She hung up. He didn't know it because he was watching the commotion across the street. Half a dozen men were pulling a cab driver from his car, the driver was dark-skinned, wore a turban and a beard. The men were all blaming the driver. Martin ran over to the scene; he said, "Wait, don't," and someone said, "What, you love these sand-niggers?"

And the cab driver with the turban was shrieking, "Fuck you! Fuck you Americans! You had this coming!"

Martin found himself kicking the cab driver. The cab driver was bleeding; his teeth were on the street.

He hadn't felt so good in months.

Now That I Know What Happened, Could You Hold Me, Please, and Say this is Love?

All, everything that I understand, I understand only because I love.

---Tolstoy

I.

I was between jobs and I felt just awful. Karin wasn't happy. We were surviving on her paychecks. It's not easy for two people to live on one income.

I was sitting in my car, smoking a cigarette and sipping from a half-pint of Teacher's. The car was parked in the grocery store lot. Karin had given me two $20 bills and said, "Go get us some groceries, enough for the week, so we won't starve to death." She always sent me grocery shopping. I was good at finding the best bargains and stretching a buck.

You get skilled at this sort of thing when you've been broke all your life. I'd been poor going on thirty-five years. It's a condition you slowly learn to embrace and accept.

I was sitting there in my car, smoking and drinking and dreading the idea of going inside the store because I would have to interact with people. I was feeling anti-social because I was feeling like shit. The only money I had in the world was $40 my girlfriend made working her ass off and I was a lazy bum who spent most of his time drinking and smoking.

Someone knocked on my window; a man in a long dark wool jacket, holding two grocery bags. He looked familiar.

"Paul?" he said.

"Hey," he said, "Paul Augustine, it *is* you."

I rolled down the window and let the smoke out.

"Jeff," I said.

"I thought that was you," he said. "What are you doing here?"

I said, "Eggs, milk, apples, hamburger meat."

"I know what you mean," he said.

I got out of the car and shook Jeff's hand. He was two inches taller than me. I never liked standing next to people who are taller than me. It was cold out. Jeff was smart to wear that wool jacket.

"Actually," Jeff said, "I was thinking of going over to the bar and having a couple of beers before heading home." He nodded his head at the small dive bar across the street.

"I'm in no real hurry to go home," he said.

"Home is where the home is," I said.

"I like that, it's profound," Jeff said. "Hey, wanna join me? I'll buy you a beer and we can catch up."

"If you're buying, I'm sittin' and listenin'."

***

There were four people in the bar. Jeff and I were two of them, the bartender was the third, and a skinny woman in her fifties was the fourth. She was drinking white Russians and playing with the ice cubes like they were the most fascinating ice cubes in the whole universe.

Jeff bought a pitcher of something on draft. I wasn't picky about beer; free is good.

"So tell me what's new," he said.

I said, "Same ol'."

He nodded. "I know the same ol'."

"You're still married to…"

"Lisa."

"Lisa."

"Yes."

"That's nice."

86

"It's not nice."

"I'm sorry," I said.

"It's marriage," he said. "We'll live."

"A toast!" I said. We toasted to marriage.

"And you," Jeff said, "the last time I saw you, you were with Rachel."

"Rachel left for Alaska."

"Why Alaska?"

"That's what I asked. She wanted to get as far away from Santa Cruz as possible. And me. I'm living with a woman named Karin."

"Karin?"

"You don't know her. She's from Albuquerque. She came out here with her husband, her ex-husband. He's a grad student at the university. Cultural anthropology, can you believe that? Something about Indians around here and ethnographies. She lives with me. Or I live with her."

"You live together," Jeff said.

"That we do," I said.

"Still writing?" he asked.

"I scribble."

"Poetry? Short stories?"

"This and that. I've been writing plays the past two years."

"Theater!"

"One gets produced now and then."

"In New York? L.A.?"

"Here. Small theaters. Black boxes with forty seats."

"Well, that's something," he said. He nodded and drank his beer.

"Isn't that something," he said.

"It is something," I said.

We drank and drank. We were on a third pitcher within the hour. Jeff couldn't handle beer the way I could. He was getting trashed; I was getting warmed up.

There was something I needed to get off my chest. I didn't realize it until that moment. I needed to tell someone. I have found that when you require another person to confess your sins to, it's better if they are drunk because they won't remember what you told them.

"I love Karin," I said, "I adore her, but I've been cheating on her."

"You have something on the side?"

"In a manner of speaking."

"How long has this been going on?"

"Three months now," I said. "The thing is this other woman, she's a married woman. She has a husband."

"So you're the other man," Jeff said, "and she's having an affair."

"It would seem to be that way."

"And your girlfriend, she has no idea?"

"If she did, she wouldn't be my girlfriend," I said.

"This sounds complicated."

"Sometimes it feels complicated."

"Who is this married woman?" he asked.

"I was teaching a poetry workshop at the adult center," I said. "A volunteer thing. I've published a few poems in literary journals so I guess they thought I could teach it. I had seven students. She was one of them."

"Sleeping with a student," Jeff said. "Is that…is that ethical?"

"Is sleeping with a married woman?"

We were on our fourth pitcher. Jeff was slurring and could barely stand. I was feeling fuzzy.

"Speaking of married women," he said, "I crossed paths with Jennifer Crane."

The name was like a washabi sword in my chest.

"Jennifer."

"You remember her?"

"Of course I do."

"Yeah, yeah, you dated her for a while."

"For a year," I said, very softly and into my beer.

"She looked good. She looked happy."

"That's it?"

"She said she just got married."

"Good for her."

"She asked about you. She did. She asked: 'How is Paul? Have you talked to Paul lately?' I told her I hadn't seen you in years."

"So she looked happy?"

"She seemed happy," Jeff said, "you know, happily married. You know, I always wanted to sleep with her. Hope you don't mind. She's pretty. What happened between you two?"

"This and that," I said. I thought about her smile. I thought about the miscarriage and the life we could have had.

***

I helped him across the street to his car. The grocery store was closed. It was a lot colder out and I just wanted to go home and get into bed with Karin and feel her warm body next to mine.

"You can't drive," I told him. "Want me to take you home?"

"Nah," he said, "I'll sleep it off in the car."

"You sure?" I said.

"No prob," he said.

I helped him into the driver's side. He slouched over and was out. He snored. He had a grin on his face. I noticed the two grocery bags in the back. What I was thinking, what I was going to do, it made me feel just awful, but I *was* awful, so I did it. I opened the back door, grabbed his bags, put them in my car, and went back home to Karin.

It was late. We'd been in that bar for hours. I watched the cloud of cold breath coming out of my mouth and the effect was hypnotic. I walked into the apartment and it was dark and quiet. Karin was in bed and she was asleep. I put the groceries away in the kitchen. Jeff had bought almost the same stuff I would've bought. In my head, I calculated that it was probably $32 worth. I still had the $40. Sometimes you get lucky. I knew I was a shit because I felt absolutely no guilt. I thought about Jennifer again and the lost baby and traced back all the events of the past six years that brought me to the life I was living.

I took a piss and went to bed with Karin and snuggled with her. She made a soft sound. I kissed her and she turned and kissed me and then we made love for half an hour and she went back to sleep and I held her, my eyes open, staring at the clock, watching the hours go by until morning. She had to wake up and go to work and earn money for the both of us.

II.

Karin was naked and drying herself off, fresh from the shower and getting ready for her day. I was still in bed and all I could do was stare at her wet pubic hair.

"You were gone for a long time last night," she said. She looked at herself in the mirror on the back of the bedroom door.

"You had beer on your breath when you fucked me," she said.

"You didn't seem to mind," I said.

"Where did you get money for beer?"

"$32 of groceries, I had a little left over."

"So you spent it on *beer?*" She turned around and gave me one of those looks that can make a man feel three feet tall.

"Are you going to give me a hard time?"

She said, "Are you going to look for a job today?"

"You know I will, you know that I am," I said. "Why do you doubt my integrity?"

She shook her head and then she shook a fist at me.

"I never doubted your integrity," she said. "I just wonder if you realize how serious our situation is."

"I know; I realize."

"I understand you're depressed," she said.

"I'm not," I said.

"Getting a job, being busy with a job, two jobs, well," she said, "you'll feel better about things. Most people do."

I watched her put on a pair of panties, and then a bra, and then a pair of faded jeans, and then a t-shirt, and then a sweater.

"Well," she said, "I'm off to clean houses and predict futures."

Karin had two part time jobs: from eight in the morning until two p.m., she worked for a cleaning service, going from house to house all over town, mostly weekly regulars; then she had two hours to herself, when she could get lunch and run errands, and from four to eight p.m. she worked at a phone psychic hot line. She was good with the Tarot cards and the runes. She would do either job full time but she liked the two hours off in between. She couldn't see herself sitting behind a phone eight hours a day, or cleaning for nine.

She gave me a kiss on the nose and I slapped her ass when she turned. She let out a small yelp.

She left and I went back to sleep.

***

Around noon I went to a bar several blocks away and looked at the classified section of the paper. It was two pages long and most of the available jobs were warehouse work, housecleaning, and landscaping. I saw an ad that said: "Are you intuitive? Can you predict the future? Psychic hotline needs phone counselors, hourly, paid weekly."

It was the same place Karin worked.

After my third vodka tonic, I started to feel guilty. I didn't like the way that feeling sat in my gut. I had $30 left and I had lied to my girlfriend. I had allowed an old acquaintance to buy me beer and then I stole from him.

"Another?" asked Bill, the bartender.

"Why not," I said, "I'm just a shit."

"What's that?"

"I'm an asshole, Bill, a real shitheel."

He placed a fresh vodka tonic in front of me. "We all are. It's just the way it is. This one is on the house, asshole."

I decided I had to make amends and come clean.

"Hey," I said.

"What, shitheel?"

"You got the White Pages here?"

"Do maggots like dead bodies?"

***

I didn't know or remember where Jeff lived. I found an address for Jeff and Lisa Bonfils about three miles away. I drove over there. It was 1:30 in the afternoon. I wasn't sure what I was going to do. Maybe I'd leave the $30 in the mailbox.

Someone was home. The door was open and the screen door locked. I could hear soft jazz playing on a radio and I could smell someone cooking tamales or tacos or something Mexican.

I rang the doorbell. A tall, slender woman with dark skin came to the door.

"Lisa?" I said.

"Yes?" she said. She looked at me with nervous suspicion. She wore jeans and a halter and an apron. She was holding a towel.

"Do I know you?" she said.

"Paul Augustine," I said.

"Oh yes. You're friends with my husband. Right? We're met before."

"Yeah, Jeff. Is he around?"

"No."

"Is he at work?"

"No."

"Will he be back soon?"

"No," she said.

"Listen," I said.

"What is it that you want?" She started to cry. "What…"

We stared at each other.

"Are you okay?" I asked.

She unlocked the screen door, wiping her eyes with the back of her hand. "Sorry. I don't mean to be rude. Come in. Please."

I hesitated. I walked in. The smell of the food was strong and it reminded me that I was hungry.

"I don't know where Jeff is," she said. "He went out last night and never came home. He was only supposed to be gone for half an hour. We were going to watch our favorite show. But he never came home. I don't know what to do. I called everyone we know. He didn't show up at work. I called family. Maybe something happened and he had to take care of it. No one has heard from him. I called the police but they said they couldn't do anything until after twenty-four hours. You know what the cop said to me on the phone? He said: 'Does your husband have a mistress?' Can you believe that? Jeff does not have - *he does not have one of those*. He is not that type of man. If he was, if he - if he was, he would be. Oh. I don't know what to do. Do *you* know where he is? Is that why you're here? Did he send you here to give me a message?"

She was a wreck. I was about to tell her I saw him last night, he got drunk, he passed out, but I knew that would open a floodgate of questions and she'd probably blame me for Jeff's drinking.

"No," I said to her, "I haven't seen him in a while, a long time, that's why I came over. I mean, I was in the neighborhood, I'm starting a new job near here, so I thought I'd drop by and say hello."

She stared at the floor. "I see. Well, he's gone missing. I couldn't go to work. I've been here all day going crazy and the only thing I can do to keep my mind off things is cook. I'm sorry...can I offer you something to drink? Water, soda? Milk? Beer?"

"No thank you."

"Would you like some lunch? I have a lot of food."

"No thank you, that's very kind," I said, "but I have to go, I'm starting a new job. I don't want to be late. I'm sorry to hear about Jeff. But look, there has to be a perfectly good explanation. He'll come back home, I'm sure of it."

"He better."

"It'll be okay."

"Paul?"

"Yeah."

She rushed toward me. She grabbed me and hugged me. She cried into my chest.

"Just hold me for a moment," she said.

So I held her. What was I going to do?

I touched her neck, her hair. "It'll be okay." My cock started to get hard and that was not a good thing.

"Tell me he's coming back home."

"He's coming back home."

"Tell me again that everything will be perfectly fine and I don't need to worry."

"Everything will work out," I said. I wanted to hit myself in the face.

"Everything will be all right," I said.

She said, "Do you promise?"

"Promise," I said. "Pinky promise."

She let go of me, wiped her eyes. "Thank you," she said.

***

I stopped off at the first bar and had a double shot of tequila and a beer chaser. The place was a stripper joint. There was one sad-looking girl on stage; she looked half asleep and didn't put much effort into shaking her skinny ass and tiny breasts. Another girl sat by the stage, sipping from a Seven-Up can. There were three customers in the place, and I made the fourth,

I thought about Jeff and wondered what the hell happened and if it was my fault. I thought about Jennifer and the life I could have had. I thought about Karin and how terrified I was of losing her. I wanted to see her immediately. I had to.

***

It was 3:00 when I got to the building where the phone psychics worked. I sat in the car and waited. I would see her before she started her shift. I would hug her and kiss her and tell her how much I loved her and how I wanted everything to work out and how it would work out and how everything about our relationship would be okay.

I waited an hour. I waited until 4:30. Her car didn't pull into the parking lot. I waited until 4:45. Maybe she parked somewhere else. I got out and went into the building.

There was a receptionist at the front of their office suite: COSMIC ADULT ENTERTAINMENT. Karin had told me the office was divided into three sections: the psychic phone line, the straight sex phone line, the gay sex phone line.

The receptionist was a plump redhead with large hair and large blue eyes. She was filing her nails.

"Can I help you?"

"Is Karin in?"

"Who?"

"Karin Wilson."

"Oh. Karin. No. She called in sick."

"She did?"

"This morning. Why do you ask?"

"Oh, well," I said, "she told me you were hiring."

"We are. You want to apply?"

"I need a job."

She handed me a clipboard with an application. "Just fill this out. Which line are you applying for?"

"I'm terrible at phone sex," I said. "As for the real thing…"

She smiled. "I bet you're a psychic."

"That I am."

"You look intuitive."

"Do you have a pen?" I asked.

She handed me a red pen. "All yours, buddy."

I sat down in the one chair across from her and filled out the application.

HAVE YOU EVER BEEN CONVICTED OF FRAUD?
No.
HAVE YOU EVER BEEN CONVICTED OF A FELONY?
No.
WOULD YOU CALL YOURSELF INTUITIVE?
All the time.
PLEASE CIRCLE WHICH TOOLS YOU USE:
TAROT

RUNES
I-CHING
MEDIUM
SPIRIT GUIDES
PAST LIVES
MONEY
LOVE
CAREER ADVICE

I circled them all and handed the application, pen and clipboard back to the receptionist.

"You can keep the pen," she said. "You look like you need a gift."

"Why, thank you."

"The manager will look this over and give you a call."

"Thanks."

"And when Karin comes in tomorrow, should I tell her you stopped by?" she said.

"Please," I said.

"Good luck."

"You too."

***

Outside, I walked to the payphone on the street corner and called home. I wanted to find out what was wrong with Karin, ask if there was anything I could get her. She didn't answer.

She wasn't there when I got home. I sat down and turned on the TV.

6:00.

Maybe she and Jeff ran off with each other, I thought.

I picked up the phone and called Terrie. Hopefully she'd answer. If her husband answered, I would hang up.

She answered.

"I was just thinking of you," she said, "how funny is that? Did you pick up on it?"

"Did I ever tell you I'm psychic?" I said.

"You're on my mind a lot lately. Did you put a spell on me?"

"How are you?"

"Missing you," she said. "Mark is out of town tonight. Medical seminar in Scottsdale."

"Right," I said, "of course."

She had told me he would be and I had forgotten.

"Do you want to see me, Paul?"

"It's why I'm calling."

"Good," she said, "good."

III.

Terrie said, "I'm always happy when I'm here with you."

Here was a motel room located in town between my apartment and her house. It was a cheap, skanky place; perfect for two people to meet and have a secret love affair. She wouldn't allow me to come over to her house, even if her husband was out of town, and she didn't feel comfortable at my place. We'd had sex once on my bed and she said she could smell Karin the whole time. In the motel room, it was another story. "Here," she said, "I feel like a different person, I do things I would never do, I feel adventuresome and I feel nasty."

I was watching the motel TV and Terrie was looking at her body in the bathroom mirror. She touched her breasts, her stomach; she turned and examined her ass. She was thirty-eight years old.

"Am I sexy?" she asked me from the bathroom.

"You know you are."

"I had a different body fifteen years ago," she said.

"We all did."

"I don't like getting old, Paul."

"It's not so bad."

She continued to stare at her body. "Sometimes I think I'm living the wrong life," she said. "This isn't the life I was destined for, but the stars were not fixed. Free will got in the way. I made the wrong choice and things changed. The future changed. Do you ever feel that way?"

I didn't have an answer for her.

She jumped on the bed and wrapped her arms around me, snuggling her face into my armpit.

"Do you love me?" she asked.

I didn't have an answer for her.

"Paul."

"What do you think?"

"I want to hear it."

"I love you."

"You're a liar."

"I love you," I said and it could have been the truth.

"In some other life, we met earlier and we got married and we're happy," she said.

"We're not happy now?"

"This is a different kind of happy," she said.

"You know what," she said, "that should be the title of your next play: *Happiness*."

"Good title."

She sniffed me. "I love the stink of a fresh sex. Let's take a shower together."

We made love in the shower. After that, we got dressed and walked across the street to the 24-hour diner for pancakes and eggs. It was 11:00 p.m.

I asked Terrie about the conference her husband was attending.

"Mark and his business partner are trying to sell that thing they invented," she said.

"The thing," I said.

"The invention," she said.

Her husband was in the medical instruments profession. He designed things and got patents and made money. He made very good money. I had never seen their house but I know it cost a bundle with two stories and had five bedrooms. Someone at the theater told me this. Terrie was on the board of directors. I never thought she was serious about poetry. The theater had produced two of my plays and would produce another if I ever wrote one. Terrie helped keep the lights on and the doors open. She once told me she hadn't had a job for the past five years because of her husband's money.

"I can never understand the things he invents," she said, "but who knows, maybe one day he'll save the world."

"And then think of the money that would make," I said.

She reached across the table and took my hand in hers and said, "I can buy a yacht and together we'll take off and sail around the world. How does that sound?"

"Sounds good."

"It's a plan then."

"You promise? Pinky promise?"

"People should never make promises because no one ever keeps them."

"Maybe that's what's wrong with the world," I said.

"Living the wrong life?" she said.

"Nobody's word is worth a damn," I said.

"Never promise anything and then things will run smoothly," she said.

"I'll keep that in mind."

She paid for dinner, like she paid for the motel. We returned to the room and indulged in oral sex. Then she went back home and I went back to the apartment.

IV.

In the kitchen, I poured tap water into a plastic cup and looked at the bedroom door. It was 2:30 a.m. Karin's car was in her parking spot. I played with the motel room key in my pocket. The apartment was very quiet. The wood floors creaked under my feet.

I undressed and got into bed. I snuggled against her. She made that small sound she always makes when our bodies touched in this way. I didn't wake her up for sex but I did wake her up.

"You're home," she said.

"It's always good to be home."

"Out drinking again, bad boy."

"Are you all right?" I asked in the dark.

"Um?"

"How was work?"

"Work is work."

"Any good predictions?"

"Um?"

"Did you save the world?"

"What are you taking about?"

"How was your day?"

"My day was long and hard," she said, "I worked. Did you work?"

Something was heavy in my chest.

"I'm tired. I want to sleep," she said.

When she got out of the shower, I was sitting on the edge of the bed and waiting for her.

"Good morning," she said.

"Morning," I said.

She gave me a kiss.

I said, "How was your day yesterday?"

"What? Why do you ask?"

"To show that I care."

"Do you *really* care?"

"I always do."

"Well," she said, "my day yesterday was like any other day."

"How so?" I said.

"I worked," she said.

"All day?" I said.

"Like any other day. You're acting strange, Paul," she said.

"No I'm not," I said.

"Yes you are. Did you take something?"

"Do you have anything to tell me?"

"Yes I do," she said. "Please go find a job. *Please.*"

***

Ten minutes after Karin left, I drove to the motel. I had the key and the room was still good until 1:00 p.m. I turned on the TV and got into bed. Terrie showed up an hour later and we fucked until noon, checked out, and went to get lunch at the same place we got dinner.

"Don't order the same thing you had last night," Terrie said.

"Best pancakes in town," I said.

"Drives me crazy," she said.

"Pancakes?"

"Patterns," she said. "We go to the same motel room, we go to the same place to eat, we order the same stuff, we sit in the same booth and we talk about the same things. Do you know I'm talking about when I talk about patterns? *Molds.*" She slammed her fist down. "This *isn't* what I want, Paul."

"What do you want?" I asked.

She thought about that and she said, "The life I was supposed to live. The one that I was destined for; the one I miss so very much."

She started to cry and with that. Everything was decided.

V.

Karin was on the phone - or in the process of calling someone - when I walked into the apartment that night. She seemed surprised, if not annoyed. She had a glass of red wine and a lit cigarette. She seldom smoked. She only smoked when something was wrong.

"Hey," she said.

"Hey," I said.

"How goes it?" she said.

"Who were you talking to?"

"Talking?"

"Phone."

"No one."

"No one?"

"Wrong number."

She was acting nervous and I didn't blame her. I nodded at the glass of wine and asked if there was any more.

"Yeah, I got two bottles. Help yourself," she said, "you will anyway."

I walked into the kitchen and poured myself some red wine. I don't normally care for red wine or wine at all but it was the only alcohol and I knew I was going to need a drink because I was going to tell her the truth; about everything.

I sat down next to her. She reached for a kiss but I didn't kiss her.

"What? You don't want to make out and get randy?"

"How was work?" I asked.

"Why do you keep *saying* that?"

"Did you do your phone psychic thing?"

"Such a funny question," she said.

"It's not," I said. I told her about yesterday, about going by her work, and her not being there.

She drank the rest of her wine and said, "I see."

"Karin," I said, getting ready to confess.

"I owe it to tell you the truth," she said. "I was having sex with someone."

I said, "Sex."

She said, "Fucking."

I asked, "With who?"

"One of my clients," she said. "Not at the hotline. A client. A man whose house I clean. He's recently divorced. He's forty-eight and he has money, a great job, I mean he's an investment banker and he has money and he says he will buy me things, he will buy me a new car and a new watch and he will get me my own apartment. I would never have to worry about rent or I could come live with him in his house."

I wasn't expecting this.

"I'm sorry," she said.

"How - how long has this been going on?" I asked.

"A month, give or take."

"Give or take what?"

She stood up.

"Paul, I'm sorry. I don't know what to do or say."

"You know where I've been? Where I go all the time?"

"Paul."

"I've been fucking someone else too. Remember Terrie Donovan? She's on the theater board. Remember her?"

"Yeah."

"I've been sleeping with her," I said, "for three months now."

"Oh, Paul," Karin said, "you're just saying that to get back at me. To get the upper hand. I'm the one who messed up."

"I've been cheating on you and it's not the first time."

"I don't believe you."

"And why is that?"

"I just don't."

"What? You don't think another woman would find me attractive?"

We didn't need to speak anymore. I sat there as she gathered a few items into a knapsack and left. I didn't ask where she was going. She didn't say goodbye but she did leave the second wine bottle, which I drank. Then I threw up.

VI.

In the morning the phone rang and I thought it was Karin but it was a man named Boyd Flemming, the manager of Cosmic Adult Entertainment.

"Mr. Augustine," he said, "I have your employment application in front of me. So you say you're psychic? You say you want to work my phone lines?"

"Sure."

"Give me a brief reading over the phone. Are you there? Are you awake?" he said. "Do you need time to get ready or are you ready now to give me a reading?"

"Sure."

"I'm ready if you're ready," he said.

I paused for what I thought would be dramatic effect. Karin had told me enough about her job so that I knew what to say: "Someone in your life, someone close to you, has lied to you. They are not being truthful. You might suspect this. Trust your instincts. Listen to your dreams because your guardian angel is trying to tell you something. Look for the number 43, it has significant meaning. And watch your diet - you need more fiber, and more greens."

"Hmm."

"Any questions?"

He asked "Is my wife cheating on me or is she faithful?"

I said, "You're not married."

"Hey, you're good."

Karin had told me he was recently divorced and that he had cheated on her.

"Your girlfriend," I said, "loves you very much."

"Not bad, not bad. When can you start?"

"When?" I said.

"Today?" he said.

"Sure," I said.

"Be here at three o'clock," he said.

***

Three o'clock. I wondered what would happen when Karin got there. I was given a phone, a small cubicle and a metal folding chair to sit on.

"The calls come in, you answer, you do your thing," Flemming said. "But keep them on the phone longer than the reading you gave me. Ten minutes is the minimum. Longer is the key. The longer they're on, the more you'll be paid above your base. You'll be here until eight. Three to eight is your shift for the next two weeks. You do good, you can go full time and have whatever shift you want."

I sat there. The phone would ring and I would answer and I would make up things, telling people on the other end that they would soon meet their soul mate, find happiness, get that job they wanted; soon their children would come to their senses and stop being delinquents. I predicted babies and grandchildren and money and happiness in the sun shiny days over yonder.

More than once I said, "Rays of sunlight will indicate that God is looking down on you and smiling."

I felt guilty. Who the hell was I to get these poor folks' hopes up? I mean, what about my needs and unhappiness? Why wasn't there someone assuring me that all would be okay?

It was a fucked up world and it wasn't going to get any better. How did I know this? Karin never showed up for work. Four o'clock - no Karin. Three other women and a man arrived. Five, six, seven - no Karin.

"Time's up," Flemming said to me at eight. "You seemed to be doing well, Mr. Augustine. Tomorrow, three o'clock."

I think he lived there at the office.

***

Everything Karin owned was gone. I walked into an almost empty apartment. She took the TV. It was her TV. At least she left the radio. Any other guy would have gone out to get shit-faced drunk but I just got into bed, turned on the radio and stared at the wall. The bed smelled like her. I couldn't sleep; she wasn't there to cuddle against.

I always hated this part.

***

Two weeks later, I was full-time at the phone psychic line. Karin never did show up and I didn't ask anyone about her; I didn't want anyone to know I was connected to her. I hoped I would hear gossip but none of the other phone workers talked about her. They didn't say much, actually. You talk for hours on the phone that when break time comes around, you enjoy the silence.

It was a good thing I had a job now because I was alone in the apartment. The job barely covered the rent with enough left over for food, beer, gas, and maybe a movie now and then. I didn't care much for movies, but Karin had taken off with the TV, and I loved TV.

I worked six days a week. I would have worked seven if Flemming let me. I thought of getting a part-time job at night. The days just blended in together and I would do anything to forget about myself.

***

"I think I'm the child of Satan," a man on the phone said, and he went into a two-hour monologue about his horrid childhood, how he was molested, how he killed people's pets and drank their blood; how he entertained fantasies about the women who lived in his building. I never said a word; just listened. When he was done, he asked, "Now, Mr. Psychic, tell me: will I rule the world in the near future, just like it says in the Bible?"

I told him yes. He was happy. I always pleased the customer.

"He left me," said a crying woman, and for the next hour she told me her life story, about her true love, how they married and stayed married for twenty years and had two children and now he was gone and living with a younger woman.

"Tell me…will he come back?"

I said yes. She sighed.

"I know he won't," she said softly, "but thank you for telling me that he will."

"I'm going to kill myself," said a young man on the phone, and for an hour and a half he told me about his crappy life; about the kids who picked on him at school, the girl who would never love him, the dreams he had of going to Hollywood and being a great filmmaker like Billy Wilder or Orson Welles.

"I would make movies," he said, "and become famous, and show them all, I'll show them all, they'll be sorry, they'll rue the day!"

I reminded him that some believed revenge was a dish best served cold.

"Hey, you're *right*," the kid said, "you know, *you're right*. I'm not going to kill myself. I'm going to become a success and show them all! Thanks, man, thank you, *you saved my life*."

***

Amber was still a kid - eighteen or nineteen - and moved from the phone sex line to the psychic one. She was small and pretty and had one green eye and one blue. She was the best woman to look at in the office, from where I was sitting. We'd smile at each other now and then but I knew I was too old for her. Driving home one night, I saw her sitting at the bus stop. I pulled up.

"Hi," she said.

"Need a ride?"

"It's okay," she said. "The bus is just late. It's always late, but not this late."

"Sometimes they break down," I said. "It's no problem. I'll give you a ride."

"Okay," she said.

She told me where she lived, five miles from where I lived. We drove for a while and I asked if she wanted to go to a bar and get a nightcap.

"Love to," she said, "but I can't go into a bar."

"A.A.?"

"Under age."

"How old?"

"Nineteen."

"How long have you been working at…"

"Enough with the questions. I could still go for a beer."

I stopped off at a liquor store, bought a six-pack, and parked somewhere away from the main street, where a cop wouldn't get curious.

We drank and chatted and it was nice.

"Being a psychic is better than being a whore on the phone," Amber said. "Oh, baby, how big are you? You know how I like it biiiiig," she said in a silly and sexy porno movie voice.

"Ever get any women calling wanting a lesbian thing?" I asked.

"You know what I have to do on the phone a lot?"

"What?"

"The fake orgasm." She let out a loud moan. "Ohhhhhhhh, baaaabbbeeeee!" and screamed out an orgasm. "What do you think?"

"Wow," I said.

"Know what I think?" she said.

"No," I said.

"I think we should go to your place where you can give me a real orgasm."

"Are you sure?" I asked.

She laughed at that. "I know what I want," she said.

VII.

Amber was wearing a tiny bikini and she looked very sexy, I must say. I wasn't the only one who noticed. Every man at the beach eyed her, even the two boys who were play-fighting and kept saying, "I'm gonna kill you, fucker, I'm gonna kill you dead like a slant-eyed nip!" I didn't mind. I liked watching them watching her. I liked watching her. She kept waving at me. She kept saying, "Come on in the water, Paul!" I shook my head. She splashed in the ocean, only going knee-deep, and she waved and said, "Come on, baby!"

Twice, a man moved near her, to join her in the water, and she moved away from him and yelled at me, "Come on, baby, before I get raped or something!"

It was enough that I was sitting there on the beach in my swim trunks and my pale skin and slight beer gut, but to get up and draw attention to myself? My skinny legs?

I had made this comment when Amber suggested we drive out to the beach.

She said, "Oh sugar you look just fine, you look better than most men and so what."

So what. I finally went into the water. I brought the flask with me. The flask was filled with Teacher's. Amber was happy that I had the flask.

"I love the ocean!" she said. "All this water."

"You remind me of a peacock," I said.

"A what?"

"Strutting your stuff."

"Hey," she said, wiggling her behind, "I have it. I'm proud of it. Why not flaunt it?"

True. I drank from the flask.

"And it's all yours," she said, grabbing me between the legs. "You should feel lucky."

"I know I'm lucky," I told her, and this was true.

I knew that later I would be sunburned and hungover and in pain.

In the car, Amber was a little drunk and she wanted to fool around. She took her bikini top off and let me play with and suck on her tiny breasts. A man my age shouldn't be with a girl so young but I figured, what the hell. She liked me, right?

I said, "This is crazy, people will see us."

"I'm crazy, baby," she said, "*crazy about you*, sugar."

My cock began to rise inside the swimming trunks. She saw this and said, "Let me say hello to my little friend." She leaned toward my crotch and grabbed me. "Not so little anymore, are we?"

We were about to do it in the back seat like we were both fifteen and skipping school for the day. Then she stopped.

She started to cry.

"Amber," I said, "What is it? What's wrong?"

"I can't do this to you," she said, crying even more. "I'm a terrible person, Paul. I feel just awful about this and that."

"I don't understand."

"I planned to use you," she said. "But you're so sweet. You're such a nice guy. You're about the best guy I've ever known and most guys are just shit and I can't do this to you."

"What?" I said. "What?"

She sat up.

"I'm pregnant," she said.

I said, "What?" again because we'd only had sex twice in the past week.

"Not yours, silly, but I was going to say it was yours," she said. "The real father, that bastard, when I told him, he said, 'Goddamn you.' And that was the last I heard from him. I'm five weeks, Paul. I was going to fuck you for a few weeks and tell you that it was yours so you would either help me pay for an abortion or marry me and start a family."

I said, "Oh."

She said, "I'm a bad person."

I said, "Not really."

She said, "Do you hate me?"

I said, "I like you a lot."

Then we had sex.

Fifteen minutes later, she said, "I don't know what to do."

VIII.

She was nervous at the clinic. She held my hand.

"I'm scared," she said.

"I'm here," I said.

"Thank you for coming with me."

***

Amber got into bed and went to sleep. In the middle of the night, she woke me up. She was crying. She cried until morning.

***

She walked away from me.

I watched her until she was gone.

She didn't show up for work the next day.

She never returned.

IX.

Two nice things happened to me in the same month. A literary journal in San Francisco published a one-act play of mine; I had mailed it out on a whim and the editor wrote back and said she loved my little piece of dramatic art and would print it in the next issue. Another small journal out of Nevada published three of my poems back to back.

Copies of both magazines arrived the same week. They looked and smelled nice printed on thick, quality paper. I mailed one of each to Karin because I thought she would be interested; I wanted to rub it in her face.

See how well I am getting along without you, is what I wanted to write in a note. Instead the note said: *Hope you enjoy!*

She called. Karin called.

She said, "Why did you send me this stuff?"

I said, "Because…why not."

"To make me feel bad?"

"No."

"It's over," she said, "I'm *over* you."

"Yeah," I said. What else could I say?

"I hate you," she said and hung up.

What else could she say? I didn't blame her.

Fifteen minutes later she called back and said, "Sorry, I'm sorry, I didn't mean that, I didn't mean to be mean. I don't hate you."

"I know."

"You don't know anything. Do you know that I actually miss you? Tell me, do you know that my heart is broken?"

"No," I said.

"You don't know *anything*," she said.

We agreed to get together and catch up. We met at a bar near her place. We had a few beers and didn't talk about anything significant. She asked if I was seeing anyone and I said no. I didn't ask about the man with the house and money because it didn't appear that she was with him; she wasn't living in his house and she was working eight hours a day as a clerk at a grocery store.

From the bar we walked back to her studio apartment. It felt like nothing bad had ever happened between us. I wanted to tell her to come back home so things would be okay again. I thought that would be a very good thing.

Her place was so small it made me feel two feet tall.

She had beer in the fridge. This was different; she never drank beer at home. At bars and parties, sure, but it was always wine at home.

I could still taste the red wine from the night she left me. I mentioned this to her.

"Are you going to get melodramatic on me?"

I said, "No."

She said, "Was this a mistake? I'm starting to think this is a mistake. I do miss you, I missed you, I wanted to see you, I wanted to see what you looked like and you look the same, maybe five pounds lighter. You smell the same. I have no idea what I'm doing. What am I doing? Do you know what's going on inside my heart? You don't know. How *could* you know? My life is different now because of you. I won't say you ruined my life but I will say you changed it. But I know I changed yours. That's what happens in relationships; we change each other. That's what is good about being two people, and that's what is bad."

"I don't understand why you sent me the play and the poems. No, I do. To make me feel bad. Don't deny it. You wanted to go, 'ha ha.' You know what these things mean to me."

"I know you're alone. I can tell. You don't have anyone in your life. I can see it in your eyes. You are love-starved. I lived with you, I should know. I can see it. You need to be touched, you need a blowjob, you need to fuck; you need love like we all need love."

She said, "You're not getting anything from me, Mister, you're not getting any love because I don't have any love to give."

She said, "You want to know about me but I bet you can tell I'm alone, too. No, it didn't work out with that man with money and the house. I never thought it would. I knew all his promises were lies but I went with him anyway, I left you for him and now I'm still poor and working a shitty job and I bet you like that. I bet you like I quit school so I'll be a nobody, just like everyone else."

I said, "Karin."

She said, "Don't you 'Karin' me. What happened to that woman? What was her name? The one you were fucking when we lived together? *The married woman?* Terrie? That's her name. What happened to her? You know what. I don't want to know. I don't care. I don't give a shit. I don't want you here. I don't know why I asked you to come here."

"Did you think I asked you over for *sex?* Did you? Just like a man to think that. I don't *want* to fuck you. I *never* want to fuck you again. I hope you *do* think I asked you over for that. *I hope it hurts, I hope it breaks your fucking heart, you motherfucking fuck you.*"

I said, "Karin."

"Fuck the 'Karin' bullshit and get out."

What happened? We were getting along so well and she turned on me. I had never seen her act like that. She was being an exaggerated version of her old self.

But I knew this was not the old Karin; this was a new Karin, a Karin with more loss and pain and sadness in her life than the Karin I used to know and love.

She said, "Get out."

"Look."

She hit me. She took a swing and hit me. She hit me in the jaw and it went numb. I tasted blood.

"Get out!"

I grabbed her. I wanted to hit her too. Instead I hugged her and she hugged me back and we both began to cry. We struggled, or she did. She wanted to get away. I wouldn't let go. She kicked me. We fell to the floor. We continued to hold each other. We kissed once or twice, our tears in each other's mouths; my blood in her mouth.

We were like that for a while and it felt like hell. It felt wrong.

She said, "I need to move away. Move far away."

She said, "I think I'll move to Nevada."

She said, "That's what I'll do: move to Nevada."

I said, "What's in Nevada?"

"It's somewhere else. It's where that magazine that published your poetry is from. Maybe they will publish me, if I moved there. Prostitution is legal there. I will move and become a whore and make a lot of money selling my pussy."

She said, "You need to go."

I was about to say something and she grabbed my mouth, my lips, and said, "All I want to hear you say is, 'Yes, ma'am.'" She made my lips form the words.

She was serious.

"Get out, never come back; don't look back, because I will be watching you leave, don't look back at my face, just walk away and let me go, okay?"

"Okay."

"That's *not* what I wanted to hear."

I said, "Karin."

She closed her eyes and said, "You have to go or I will get violent again and I don't want that and you don't want that."

I stood up and left and that was the end of that part of my life.

X.

It was going to be a cold winter.

It wasn't cold yet but it was getting there and I could feel it in the air, in the future; it would three months of chilly scenes of winter and to make matters worse, I would be alone for the holidays.

I didn't want to be alone but there didn't seem to be anything to do about it because I was so that was the end of that.

I told myself: 'Accept it, Paul Augustine. You can get through the winter and Christmas alone. You've made your way through worse, son.'

I started to drink more, as if I wasn't drinking enough. I couldn't sleep either. Drinking used to put me to sleep but now, when I drank more, I just stayed awake; I would drink until the sun came up and then take a shower and go to work drunk. No one seemed to notice. No one cared. So I drank even more.

Most bars were warmer than my apartment with its thin, hardwood floors. I found myself drinking out more often, spending more money than I had.

One night, at a certain bar, I thought I saw someone I knew.

I thought it was Jeff. I imagined him telling me he went off on a grand adventure, full of heroic Campbellian motifs and themes, riddled with beautiful women and kinky sex. It wasn't Jeff. It was my former boss, Boyd Flemming. He spotted me first.

"Look what the cat dragged in," he said. He picked up his beer and sat next to me.

I didn't have a good comeback for that.

He shook my hand. He seemed to be glad to see me.

"How's it been?" he said.

"So-so," I said.

"The company was closed down by the Feds," he said, "I barely got out in time. Something about telephone fraud, interstate laws, blah blah. It was the sex lines they wanted, not the psychic. But this biz comes and goes like the clap. I'm in a better biz now. You ever heard of time shares?"

"No."

"It's all the rage."

"Good money?"

"Getting there."

"That sounds keen," I said. I wanted to go but he offered to buy me a drink and I can never turn down free booze. Which meant I had to listen to him.

That was okay, I was getting better at blocking people out. I nodded my head and smiled and nodded my head and pretended like I was listening, and then I became quite interested and listened; he mentioned Karin's name.

He said, "By the way, I knew you had a thing going with that young thing. Ashley was it? No, Audrey."

"Amber."

"Amber, that's right," he said, "I mean, did you think you were hiding anything from me? I always know what goes on. Frankly, I was happy for you. I was proud of you, getting a hot young piece of ass like that. I've gotten laid from that job. You're around women all the time, working that close. Things happen. Right? Right. So I've had my share, yes sir, I've had my fill, and I've had my regrets. Is regret the right word? There are women who worked there I wished I had gotten into the sack, I wish I had made a move on."

He listed a few names I didn't know and then he said, "and Karin."

"Karin?"

"Did you know her?"

I asked, "Karin who?"

"I don't think she was there when you were there," he said. He described her and he was talking about my Karin.

"She had a boyfriend or husband, I forget," Flemming said, "I know she was taken, but she was a looker, she had beautiful big saucer eyes and nice hair and a good ass. I wanted to make a move on her the day I overheard her talking to another girl in the break room about how she had started an affair with some man she met on her other job and how this man had money and a good job unlike her husband or boyfriend. 'He's such a bum,' I remember her saying, 'I am thinking of leaving him for this other man even if I know this other man only wants sex.' So I thought, damn, if the hot bitch is unhappy at home and looking for outside dick to put a smile on her face, I can give her what she needs. And then a week later she quit."

He talked about other women he wished he had fucked and some he did fuck and kept patting me on the back and telling me I did a good job getting into Amber's pants.

We left the bar together.

"Damn it's cold," he said.

"Yeah," I said.

"That Karin, now that I think about her," he said, "she was nothing but a horny slut and I should have nailed her ass to the door."

I turned to him and kicked him in the balls. He fell to the ground. I kicked him in the face and knocked out his teeth.

"I loved her, asshole."

I walked away, leaving him bleeding on the icy ground.

***

I wish.

What I just wrote is a lie.

He said that, he said what he said about the woman I once loved, still loved, who moved to Nevada and didn't talk to me.

He said that. I did nothing and said nothing.

"Well," he said, "have a good holiday."

"You too," I said.

We shook hands and I went home.

XI.

I never thought much about sex during the holidays; it was Christmas Eve and Olivia was supposed to come by after her show; it was closing night of a play she was in and we were going to meet for a few drinks and talk about our lives. I hadn't seen her in two years. She had acted in a play I had written. There was something between us once, the back and forth, casual glances; brief discussions of getting together for a date, then silence, then nothing.

We started talking again. She was still single, a single mother, working a 9-to-5-office job and working theater at night and dreaming the things all hopeful actresses dream of.

"We should go have a drink," she said.

I found myself looking forward to seeing her; I had visions of us picking up where we left off, recreating some sense of hope and love, and waking up together on Christmas morning, each renewed like Ebenezer, cheerful music playing in the background and her daughter like Tiny Tim, telling us all is well. God bless.

And then everything would be okay.

But her daughter was in some other state with her father. Olivia was depressed and lonely because the only person who mattered to her was away from her on that cold Christmas Eve.

It was so chilly I could see my breath in my apartment and I was wearing gloves. I had presents for her and the kid - last minute items that I went out and bought and had wrapped. It felt good to buy the gifts.

She came by my apartment after her show - she said it was a good closing night with half the house filled, which isn't bad for a closing - and we walked down the block to the bar.

There were maybe seven people in the bar, some playing pool, some sitting around. We both had White Russians. I got up to go to the bathroom, was gone maybe thirty seconds, and there was already a guy sitting next to her at the counter - he was playing pool - acting like he was going to order a drink. Twenty empty seats at the counter and he sits on the one next to her.

"Excuse me," I said.

He turned to me.

"Um."

I nodded at my drink.

He looked at my drink, then me, his eyes red, angry, like he wanted to hit me. I was ready for anything because I knew anything could happen.

He moved away.

Olivia said, "I haven't been inside a bar in a year. I forget what it can be like."

"Has he been waiting for me to go take a piss to make his move?"

"I've been on dinner dates when my date gets up for the restroom, men sitting at other tables immediately introduce themselves with flattering words. 'Oh, I just want to say, what a nice dress…your hair is very nice, I like your shoes.'"

"Jerks."

"People are lonely everywhere," she said.

We had a second drink and left the bar. Outside, a girl in a thick jacket, straight black hair and heavy eyeliner asked if we had any spare change.

"No," said Olivia.

I gave the girl a dollar.

"Thanks, man!" said the girl.

"I never give anyone change," Oliva said.

"It's Christmas."

"Yeah. Ho ho."

Back at my apartment, she didn't want to come inside, she wanted to go home, so I tried to kiss her and she kissed me back but said softly, "Did you think something was going to happen?"

I didn't know how to answer that.

"I just wanted to drop by, say hi, have a drink," she said.

"Of course," I said.

She left. I went inside and looked at the gifts. She called when she got home. "I'm sorry about that," she said.

"It's okay."

"It's not okay."

"You could come back."

"Some things have happened," she said. "I'm just not into that right now…"

***

I didn't have any booze at home. I went back to the bar. There was still an hour before last call. The girl with the black hair and thick jacket was still outside, asking for change.

"Hey," she said, "thanks for the dollar again!"

"Want a drink?"

"What?"

"Do you drink?"

"Who doesn't?"

"Wait. You old enough?"

She laughed. "Funny. I'm twenty-five!"

I had another White Russian and she had a Long Island Iced Tea and then we had two more. She said her name was Taylor and I didn't believe her. She said she had been sleeping in her car all week. She didn't go into details and I didn't need them.

"I live a block away," I said.

"I can't give it you for free," she said after a pause.

"I know."

"Just to get that out of the way."

Back at my apartment, I asked her how much.

"Um," Taylor said, rolling her eyes. She was nervous. "Let's see. Okay, look, I don't really do this so I'm not sure what the going rate is, you know, for a blowjob or a fuck or if you want to stick it in my ass..."

"How about everything?"

"How about $100."

"Deal."

"That was easy."

"I like it when it's easy."

I got out my wallet and handed her five $20s. She rolled them up and the money disappeared in her jacket like she was a magician.

In bed, her body was taut and slender from too many missed meals - that thick jacket hid her emaciated frame. Her skin was pale and goose-bumped. I held her close to me, under the blankets, until she seemed to get warm.

We kissed.

"This is nice," she said, like she was surprised.

"Yeah."

"Condoms?"

"Plenty," I said, reaching for the nightstand drawer where I had a dozen assorted brands.

"Always prepared," she said.

"Always hopeful," I said.

We fucked for a while, this position and that, she was responsive and moaning; while I had her on her stomach, she said softly, "Okay, now, stick it my asshole."

"Yeah?"

"You paid for it, boy."

"Do you want that?"

"It's what I want, now," she said, her voice changing, deeper, *"Now! Stick it in, motherfucker, just do it."*

I did and she went limp and purred.

***

She started to get dressed.

"Where you going?"

"A question filled with mystery and no answers," she said.

"Don't sleep in your car. You can stay here."

It was 7:00 a.m. and I woke up to a blowjob. It was nice to open my eyes and see a woman with my cock in her mouth. She grabbed a condom from the nightstand and moved on top of me.

"Ho ho ho," she said.

***

This time she said she really had to go when she put her clothes on. I was going to suggest breakfast but she looked a lot different in the morning light. She appeared scared and confused and I knew she didn't do this much, if ever at all; she felt ashamed and I wanted to tell her not to be. I walked her to the door.

"Wait," I said.

I picked up the two wrapped presents and handed them to her.

"Happy holidays," I said.

She didn't know what to make of this. "For me?"

"Of course."

"How…"

"I just knew."

"Thank you," she said, and she left.

I felt ashamed, but glad the presents were gone.

XII.

In two weeks, my new play, *Happiness*, would open. I didn't think it would, at least not well. The director was still fumbling with blocking, changing things at every rehearsal, and the actors were not completely off-book, fumbling with their lines.

Olivia didn't have her lines down and it was bothering me. She should know better; not only was it my play, she wasn't professional.

Then again, this was little community theater. No one was a professional. But still.

I mentioned this to her when we had dinner and some drinks after rehearsal.

"Don't worry," she said, "I'll be ready. I'm *always* ready."

"Two weeks," I said.

"Two weeks is forever," she said. "Why are you so worried?"

I didn't know. I shrugged. Shrugging was becoming a habit lately.

"Well," she said, "it is your work, these are your words I am saying on stage, so you have a right to be worried. You have a right to…"

She stopped and stared inside her glass.

She put her hand to her mouth and spit out a small shard of glass.

"What the hell," I said.

"There's another," she said, "look."

I looked, and saw a bigger shard of glass at the bottom of her glass.

"Are you okay?" I said. I was scared.

"Did you swallow anything?" I said.

"No," she said.

"Did you cut yourself?"

"No."

"Are you sure?"

"I'm sure," she said.

"Now I really have something to be worried about," I said.

"I'm okay," she said, "but thank you."

I was angry. I checked my glass. Olivia waved the waiter over, showing him the glass. He turned pale. He went to get the manager, a small, frail woman in her forties. She was upset, too. They were worried about a lawsuit. They asked Olivia if she swallowed any glass.

126

"I can call 911," the manager said.

Lawsuit, I thought. Money.

"I'm fine," Olivia said, "thank you."

"Allow me to get your dinner, on us," said the manager. "And whatever drinks you want, on the house. Drink as much as you'd like."

"Well," Olivia said, "will the glass be glass-free?"

"We have paper cups."

Olivia laughed.

We ordered more food so we could get stuffed. We switched from beer to vodka tonics.

"Too bad it's not the weekend," Olivia said. "Too bad I have to work in the morning."

"Why?"

"I could drink like a fish and get snookered beyond belief, and we could take a taxi cab home. Ella would be at her father's."

"Yeah," I said, "too bad."

We left. Olivia wanted to leave a tip but I talked her out of it. Why a tip when she could have been seriously hurt?

We stood outside the bar and grille and it was very cold. She took my hand in hers and said, "Brrr."

"If you had cut yourself," I said, "think of the money you could've made."

"Money?"

"Lawsuit."

"Oh," she said. "Damn, you're right. How much do you think I could've made? What would they have settled for?"

I shrugged. "Fifty grand, maybe a hundred."

"Boy what I could do with that kind of cash. Pay off my car, my cards, put Ella in private school." She looked at the bar and grille. "Do you have a time machine, Paul? Can we go back and I can bite down on that piece of glass and get rich?"

I tried to hold her but she stepped back. She looked very sad.

She said, "I'm just too goddamn honest for my own good."

I was about to suggest we go back to my apartment for a while but she said, "I have to get home to my baby."

Her daughter was with her mother. She kissed me, lightly.

"You know how my mother is," she said.

Her mother made me nervous.

XIII.

Olivia's mother was a psychotherapist, specializing in abnormal behavior and sexuality. At any given moment she would quote from Freud or Lacan or French guys I'd never heard of. She said she took a postmodern approach to therapy. I had no idea what that meant. She was writing a book about her theories. I was glad I wasn't one of her patients.

I think she was trying to make me one of her patients, though. She had read my plays and my published poetry.

"My mother would like to talk to you about your writing sometime," Olivia said.

"Why?"

"Why not."

"Why," I said. "Does she want to psychoanalyze me?"

"Maybe."

"Jesus," I said.

"Amuse her."

"Can I pass?"

"You can't *pass,"* she said. "She's curious, we're together now."

"Are we together?" I asked.

"Well," she said, "we're having *sex* now, so I would say so."

We only had sex on the weekends, when her daughter was in the custody of her father, Olivia's ex-husband. I wasn't allowed to spend the night when her child was home, not right now, Olivia said. And of course she couldn't stay over my place, unless her kid was at her grandmother's or her friends. But there was Olivia's job. And there were her dreams about Hollywood.

"Some day I'm going to move to Los Angeles and give Hollywood a try," she said

"When?"

"Soon."

She was twenty-eight. If she was serious about acting and Hollywood she had to do it soon.

The problem: the custody agreement with her ex- was that she couldn't leave Santa Cruz with their child, unless he agreed to it, and he was never going to agree. He was never going to take full-time custody, and she wouldn't let him. So that Hollywood dream was nothing but a dream. When Olivia accepted the fact it would never happen, she would run into a wall and do something drastic and draconian…and sad.

***

I treated the women to a nice dinner - Olivia, Ella, and Dr. Joyce Wren. Olivia assured me that it would be a good move on my part if she and I were going to get serious, if we were going to have a life together.

The dinner cost me half my paycheck but I decided it was worth it. I was planning on asking Olivia to marry me. The idea of being domestic was appealing in those days.

"This is wonderful food," Olivia said at the restaurant.

"Did you like your dinner?" she asked Ella.

Ella nodded her head, eating ice cream for dessert. She loved ice cream.

"I always adored this place," said Joyce. "Thank you, Paul."

"You're welcome, Joyce."

We were being so formal and polite. Joyce was a die-hard Republican and always wanted Olivia to marry a doctor or a lawyer, not get pregnant at nineteen.

"Paul," Joyce said, "your writing intrigues me."

"Thank you," I said. Was that the right answer? What did *intrigue* mean? Was there a hidden meaning? I was psychoanalyzing myself.

"Have you written a novel?" she asked.

"I haven't thought about it," I said, which was a lie because I had. "So many pages. So many words. I'm not sure I have that much to say."

"Well you have to write a novel to get on the bestseller list and make a lot of money, right? I mean, there is no money in writing poetry, is there? And your plays have only been produced locally."

"Mother," Olivia said, giving her a look.

"Just asking, dear."

"I don't write with any goal of being rich from it," I said.

"So why do you write?"

"Well," I said.

"Why did you become a shrink, Mother?" Olivia said. She was getting annoyed. I could tell they had had this back and forth all their lives, since Olivia was Ella's age.

"To help people," she replied, "and to make them happy."

"Writing makes me happy," I said.

"Truly happy?" she asked.

"What's happiness?" Olivia said.

"The name of Paul's new play!" Ella said.

"That's right," Olivia said, "the new play."

"How is the play going?" Joyce said.

"Good," I said.

Olivia said, "Splendidly."

"How are the audiences?"

"They seem to like it," I said.

Olivia said, "Packed houses each night!"

That was a lie. They were selling half the seats at best, and the play was closing next week.

"Well the reviews are good," Joyce said.

"Yes they are!" Olivia said proudly.

"Frankly, I wasn't sure I understood it," Joyce said, "but it was *interesting.*"

Olivia's shoulders slumped, as if she were defeated.

"Paul," Joyce said, "I wouldn't mind if we could, some time, discuss your writing. I have some questions."

"Um," I said. "Certainly, Joyce, I'd love to."

"We can pencil in a time, you can come by my office."

Olivia and I looked at each other. She laughed at our exchange and said, "What? Oh, come on, I won't *bite.*"

XIV.

Ella Wren and I got along famously. It was like we had known each other forever. I knew I could do a good job being her stepfather. I would watch her when Olivia was rehearsing another play (if she was lucky to get cast; there were a lot of actresses in town competing for the few roles around) or worked the occasional catering job to earn extra money. I would either go to their place or Olivia would drop her off at mine. I started to wonder what kind of home we could get together.

Ella and I would sit around and watch TV. She could always watch TV with me. We ate ice cream together. Olivia thought TV was bad for the mind and a waste of time - to which I asked, if she got a part on a TV show, would she turn it down? Of course not.

"We all have a price tag," she said.

I would take Ella to the movies. Olivia and I hardly went to the movies. I liked doing things with her. I liked it when people thought she was my kid. "You have a beautiful daughter," people would say.

"Why thank you," I'd say back.

Ella started calling me "fake step-dad."

***

Her real dad was an asshole. It was an unplanned marriage, they were kids, they had no business getting married or starting a family but Olivia couldn't face going through another abortion.

"I have no regrets about having Ella," she said one night when we were drinking heavily and she was being confessional. "But I know my life would be different if I hadn't. Anything is possible," she said, "anything could've happened. I know I would be in Los Angeles right now, and my life…well, who knows what the heck my life would've been like. Maybe I would've been famous by now; maybe I would've been crushed on the boulevard of broken dreams."

She also got poetic when she drank.

And she got sad when she drank.

And she never remembered what she did or said when she drank.

"What happened?" she said.

"When?" I said.

"I screwed the wrong guy and my life changed," she said, "why did I do that?"

I held her to me and she cried into my chest.

"Why can't he be a good father?" she said.

"The hell with him," I said.

He took custody of her each weekend, rather than once a month, because it meant less child support he had to pay out. I didn't understand how that all worked but it was what it was.

132

"She really likes you," Olivia said, "she's quite taken with you. She usually doesn't like the men I date."

I wanted to remind her that the men she saw in the past were all brainless thugs or jerks, but I knew better. I had no idea who they were. This is what Ella told me: "They're all big like cavemen," she said, "and they're never very smart. I don't know what my mom sees in them."

"Why is that?" Olivia asked.

"Why is what," I said. I was too occupied with my memories.

"Why is she so fond of you?" she said. "Are you fond of her?"

"You know that I am."

"I'm happy about that…"

"I adore her," I said, "I love the both of you."

"Oh, oh," she said, and she pressed her face into my chest.

"I hate what she has to go through," she said, "what she has to go through when she has to go to her father's house."

"I know," I said, and that made me very sad. "I don't like it either."

"I don't know what to do."

"We can do something."

"When I think about it," she said, "I just drink."

***

We were drinking too much when we were together. That was a revelation for me. Olivia wanted to match me drink for drink, beer for beer, the result being a bad hangover in the morning, something she blamed me for.

"Why do I drink so much with you?" she would say. "Why don't you stop me from getting drunk?"

Ella's father had remarried two years ago. His new wife did not like Ella. Ella had her own room at his house. She stayed in the room most weekends and read books. Her favorite writers were

Tolkein and Le Guin. I would read to her, out loud, passages from *Lord of the Rings* or the *Earthsea* books. Reading was her escape from the unhappiness she felt when at her dad's house. If he wasn't ignoring her, his wife was mean to her. That's what Ella said, anyway; she told her mother this, and told me that her father's wife (her 'stepmonster') was jealous. She could not conceive. They were trying to have a baby and it wasn't happening and when Ella's evil stepmother looked at Ella, she saw everything she wanted but could not have.

When I thought about Olivia's life, all I could think about was choices and the many bad ones she made.

And I thought about my many choices, my past, and when I did, I thought about Jennifer, and I thought about Karin, and I thought about Terrie; and I thought about how I hoped I wouldn't fuck things up with Olivia the way I had fucked things up before.

***

And so came the day when things got a bit messy.

It was a Saturday morning and I had a mild hangover which was not unusual. I had had varied degrees of hangovers every morning for the past fifteen years.

The doorbell rang.

Ella was there, alone, with a stuffed backpack and a heartbreaking look on her small, pink face, the sort of countenance best reserved for the most tragic of women in history.

Pain.

"Ella," I said.

"Fake stepdad," she said, walking past me and sitting on the couch, "please help me. Can you help me? I need your help."

"Where's your mom?"

"Mom...is at home."

It was 12:15 p.m. Her father picked her up at noon each Saturday, and returned her to Olivia on Monday evening, usually after school, if there was school.

I realized that Olivia did not bring her here.

"Wait a minute," I said. "You're supposed to be - what are you doing here, Ella? How did you get here?"

I sat down on the floor, looking at her, knowing there was trouble.

"Ella," I said.

"I took the bus," she said.

"What do you mean you took the bus?"

"I *know* how to get here," she said. "I told my mom that I was going to the store to get some chips and soda. She gave me some change. I used the change to get on the bus and come here."

"Why?"

"I don't want to go to my dad's," she said; her voice started to become desperate. "I *hate* it there. I really *hate it.* Can I stay here? Can I hide here? I'll just hide and my dad won't care...he'll be happy he doesn't have to bother with me."

I closed my eyes. "Oh, Ella."

"Did I do something wrong?"

"You can't do this," I said. "You're supposed to be in your father's custody. I could get in trouble, you know. I could get into a lot of trouble, you being here. It looks funny."

"What do you mean?" she asked.

"It's complicated."

"So? Tell me."

"Your father could cause trouble for me."

"I hate him."

"No you don't."

"I hate his wife then," she said.

"Your mother's is going to flip out," I said.

The phone rang.

"That's probably her."

"Don't tell her I'm here!" she said.

"I can't do that," I said.

Ella slumped in the couch. She knew I was right.

"I'm sorry, fake stepdad," she said.

"It's okay," I said and answered the phone.

"Oh God, Paul, I don't know what's going on," Olivia said. "I'm - I'm - Ella…"

"She's here," I said.

"What?"

"Ella is here."

"What the *hell* is she doing *there*?"

"Well," I said.

"My ex- is *pissed.*"

***

I drove Ella back to her home.

"Are you going to marry my mom?" she asked.

"Why do you ask?"

"Are you?"

"Do you want me to?"

"Yes."

"Would you want me to be your real step dad?"

"Can you be my *real* dad?"

That was the most pitiful question anyone had ever asked me. If Jennifer had had the baby, the child would be around Ella's age now.

"I can," I said.

"Will you marry my mom?"

"That's something you need to ask your mom."

"I think she wants you to."

"You think?"

"I never know what is going on in her mind."

"You and me both, kiddo."

"Sometimes she embarrasses me."

"That happens."

"Sometimes she makes me…."

She didn't have to say it.

"That happens," I told her.

"She cries a lot, in her room. In the middle of the night. I hear her. She cries."

I didn't know that.

"And she drinks a lot."

I did know that.

***

Olivia and her ex-husband, Dan, were waiting outside when I pulled the car up. Dan's wife was sitting in his beat-up Pinto. She wore thick glasses. She glared at me and Ella and I felt my skin start to crawl.

"Ella!" Olivia said, going to her. I could tell she was trying not to let Dan know anything. She patted Ella's backpack. "You have everything?"

"Yeah," Ella said.

She was meek in front of her father.

"What's going on here?" Dan said. "It's 12:40."

"I'm sorry, man, I'm really sorry," I told him. "I took her out to breakfast and wasn't looking at the clock."

"She's mine at noon," he said.

"I'm really sorry."

"It's not his fault, Dad," Ella said. "It's mine. I…"

"Get in the car, girl," he said.

"Dan," Olivia said.

"Ella. *Get in the car!*"

137

Ella nodded and shuffled toward the Pinto, getting in back. Dan's wife stared at us.

"What the fuck is going on here?" Dan said to Olivia.

"Don't start," she said.

"What are you trying to do? You trying to take my little girl away from me?"

"No," I said.

He got into my face. "Are we going to have a problem?"

"No," I said.

"Dan," Olivia said.

He had a smirk on his face and I wanted to slap it off him. He turned around, got into the Pinto and drove off.

I heard him say to Ella, "He is not your father!"

Olivia and I stood there. She was looking at me like...I don't know.

"This is just great, Paul, great," she said.

She went into her place. I followed her to the kitchen. She got two beers out of the fridge, handed me one. She drank half a bottle in one gulp.

"I don't need this sort of thing in my life," she said.

"I didn't do anything wrong."

"I know you didn't."

"But?"

"I don't *need* my goddamn fucking ex-husband giving me grief," she said.

"Fuck him," I said.

"I did and I got knocked up."

She finished her beer and got another.

"Olivia, it's not even one o'clock."

"So. It's my free day. I can do what I want. And I want to drink," she said.

"I want to get drunk. Is any other weekend different?" she said.

We usually didn't start drinking until later in the day, but what the hell.

"Hold me?" she said. "Paul Augustine?"

I held her in my arms and she cried.

"She's too fond of you."

"Is that a bad thing?"

She said, "I don't know."

XV.

I could hear them in their kitchen: the married couple that lived next door. She was cooking sloppy joes for dinner and they were arguing about money and bills.

"Isn't that something," Olivia said. "They're at it all the time."

"How old are they?" I asked.

"Forties or fifties," she said. "They've been married forever."

They were arguing about what they did and did not have in the bank.

"I hate you," said the woman.

"Finish making dinner and shut the fuck up," said the man.

"Oh God," Olivia said. She stuck her face into my neck and I touched her long blonde hair. I thought she was going to cry again. She did not cry again.

She said, "If I stayed married to Dan, I would have been that woman."

"The hell with your dinner!" yelled the woman. "Come and get it, asshole!"

"Crazy bitch you," said the man.

"Oh," Olivia said.

"The heck with those people," I said, "we are not those people."

139

We were in bed. We'd been drinking and making love all day and it was night. We'd drink and make love more and pretend our lives were different.

Olivia was in a mood still, after the incident with Ella and her ex-husband. We got to that point where we talked about the past, and the other people we had slept with and loved or hated.

"The boy who got me pregnant when I was fifteen, I was terribly in love with him," she said. "He was seventeen. He was the first. He was the only. I had images in my head. Bliss, happy forever, happy ending, me and him and our little baby. When I told him, when I told him I was pregnant, he said, 'Who got you pregnant?' I said, 'Who do you think?' He said, 'You're a whore.' I said, 'I've only been with you.' He said, 'I don't believe you.' He said, 'That's not my baby in your gut,' and he hit me, he hit me in the face, and then he hit me in the chest, and then he kicked me in the leg and I fell on the ground and he kicked me again and he said, 'If you tell people that it's mine, I'll kill you.' I couldn't believe this was happening. Here he was, there he was; the boy I loved and would love forever, and he was hurting me, he was kicking me and hitting me and threatening to murder me and denying that he ever fucked me - I mean, I gave my virginity to him - and I thought this was a nightmare, I thought: This cannot be happening. I thought: 'The boy I loved and who loved me would never do this, would never.' And then I knew. I knew he only said he loved me so he could get into my pants, so he could stick his cock in me, and that was all, all he wanted was pussy and he got it, and this was the price I had to pay for wanting love."

"So you had an abortion."

"I told my mother," she said. "I didn't know where else to turn. When I told her, she said, 'Oh, Olivia.' She shook her head and she sighed and she rolled her eyes and she goes, 'Oh, Olivia.' I didn't know what to do. She said, 'I know a doctor who can help.'"

I wish I knew that doctor for Amber; we wouldn't have had to go down to Tijuana.

"And then I tried to kill myself," she said.

"Sssh," I said.

"I really did want that baby," she said.

"Okay," I said, "don't…"

"I knew he was a boy," she said, "and today we would be…today he would be…today he would be in high school…"

She cried but she only cried a little. She reached for the warm beer on the nightstand.

"Your first love?" she asked.

"I had many first loves," I said. I was trying to be funny.

"Once you said," she said.

"Jennifer," I said.

"She had a miscarriage," she said.

"She did, yes," I said.

"Did you want the baby? I think you wanted the baby."

I told her about Amber and Tijuana.

"You never told me about *her*," Olivia said.

"There was no need."

"And it wasn't yours?"

"No."

"If she had given birth, would you have helped her?"

"Maybe," I said. "Probably."

"Did you love her?"

"No."

"Did you love Karin?"

"Yes."

"Did you love the married woman? Tracy?"

"Terrie."

"Did you?"

"I don't know."

"How many girls have you loved?" she asked.

"How many men have you loved?" I asked.

"I don't want to talk about it," she said.

"Why are we talking about any of this anyway?" I said.

"I don't know," she said.

"Did you ever love Dan?"

"I told myself I did, when I was pregnant," she said, "but I never really loved him, even though I married him."

"Why did you ever get together with him?"

"Because he was nice, he seemed nice," she said, "he didn't hit me, at least."

"The men in your life hit you? All of them?"

"A lot of them," she said.

"I won't ever," I said.

"I know," she said. "Have you ever hit a woman?"

"No."

"I think he hits her," she said, taking about the neighbors, who were quiet right now, but would start up again, fighting, because they always did.

"I have heard sounds," she said, "and I know those sounds. I know what it sounds like when a man hits a woman."

We made love.

We drank.

She said, "Tell me more about Karin."

I didn't want to.

"She hurt you," Olivia said.

"No," I said.

"Yes," I said.

"You loved her."

"I loved her."

"You've loved a lot."

"I love you," I said.

"I know," she said, "you weirdo."

XVI.

Olivia was talking and she was talking fast. We were having an argument. She was angry or irritated. And then she said, "What was I talking about?"

"Drinking," I said.

"Drinking," she said. "Don't you think we've been drinking too much?"

"Have we?"

"Don't you think?"

"I don't know."

"I think we have," she said.

"Why?" I asked.

"I think I'm an alcoholic," she said. "What do you think?"

"I wouldn't know."

"Are you an alcoholic?" she said.

"I've always liked to drink," I said.

"Drinking to have fun is one thing," she said. "Social drinking, drinking to celebrate - if I had anything in my life to celebrate. But I seem to be drinking to cope. To cope."

"Cope with what?"

"With everything. When I have thoughts, I need to cope and I drink."

"What kind of thoughts?"

"You know," she said, "about everything. Acting, children, life, you."

"You drink when you think about me?" I said.

"Of course I do."

"To cope with me?"

"To cope with…my thoughts."

"Is that supposed to make me feel good?" I said. "It doesn't make me feel good," I said.

143

"I get depressed because I don't know where we're going, what kind of future we have," she said. "I don't have time to fart around. Where are we going, Paul?" she said.

"This is not what we were talking about," I said.

"What, what were we talking about?"

"Drinking."

"I need another beer," she said.

We had this conversation at least once a week. Were we getting drunk too much? It always happened on the weekend when Ella was away and we could drink. We'd get drunk and talk about getting drunk. We'd agree we should cut back, and then we'd drink more and promise tomorrow would be the day we'd start drinking less but of course tomorrow was another day, another day to drink and talk and fuck and laugh and cry.

This time it was different. This time she was truly serious and I knew something was wrong.

"What's wrong?" I said.

"What makes you ask?" she said.

"I know you," I said.

"Okay, okay," she said.

"My period is late," she said.

"What?"

"Two weeks late," she said.

"What does this mean?"

"I might be pregnant," she said. "And if I am, I am going to have to stop drinking, and if I stop, I want you to stop too."

XVII.

Olivia had her period. It was a relief, of course, but she was also depressed.

"Look on the bright side," I said, "you can still continue drinking."

"That's not funny," she said.

"It *is* pragmatic," I said.

"Do you think this is fun time?" she said. "Johnny Carson ha ha."

"I thought you didn't want to be pregnant," I said.

"Only because I'm poor and I have ambitions," she said. "But I do want another baby, some time, some day, maybe soon. Maybe two more babies, maybe three. Maybe a house full of them. But I'd need a house to put them all in. I do want another one. I don't want Ella to be an only child."

"She *would* like a baby brother or sister," I said.

"Yes," Olivia said, "I know."

I could see it on her face, in her eyes. So I said, "Let's have a baby then."

"Never joke about such a thing."

"I'm not."

She could tell I was serious.

"Really?"

"Really," I said.

"You want a child?"

"We both do."

"Oh no," she said, "another illegitimate baby in the world. Does the world need another one of those?" she said.

"We'll get married," I said.

"Really?" she said.

"Really."

"You would marry me?" she said.

"I've been wanting to bring it up for a while."

"Hold me," she said.

I held her and it was nice.

"I feel safe," she said.

Took three months, but the next time her period was late it was late for real and so we were going to have a baby. We were going to be parents.

"You're going to be a father," Olivia said.

Those words sounded so distant, like they were in another language from a far away country of strange looking people. We celebrated with a bottle of champagne and a fifth of Chivas Regal. Only the best for the mother of my child.

"This is the last sip," she said. "I really have to quit drinking now. I have to be responsible."

"I love you for this," I said.

"You have to stop drinking too; you have to go through this with me," she said.

"It's only fair," she said.

I had no intention of quitting booze but I said, "Okay."

She said, "Promise?"

I said, "Promise."

"Pinky promise?"

We linked our little fingers.

"We need to set a wedding date," she said.

We sat down with her daughter and told her there was a baby coming and that we were going to get married.

"Oh," Ella said.

"This is good news," I said.

"So you won't be my fake step dad anymore?" she asked. "You'll be my real step dad?"

"I'll be your *dad,*" I said.

"He'll be a dad and you'll be a sister," Olivia said.

Ella thought about this for a minute and then she smiled.

"Family hug," Olivia said.

The three of us embraced and I thought: I am the luckiest man in the world. I felt like it.

We had no idea how the hell we were going to afford everything but that didn't seem to matter, practical things didn't seem to be real when there was love and love was more real than anything.

***

One day, Ella called on the phone and she was frantic and screaming and scared.

"Paul!" she cried. "Come here quick! I don't know what to do!"

"What is it?"

"My mom!" she said.

"What about her?"

"I think she's dead! Oh, Paul, please get here now! I'm scared!"

Ella had come home from school and saw blood all over the bathroom. There was a trail of blood to Olivia's bed and Olivia was unconscious on the bed. Ella could not wake her up. Ella did not see the empty bottle of sleeping pills on the floor, but I did.

Seeing the blood and the bottle and Olivia unconscious, I knew exactly what happened. My soul left my body.

Ella sat in the corner of the bedroom and cried.

"It's okay," I told her.

"Is...is she dead?"

"No," I said.

I got a cup of water, stepping in the blood on the bathroom floor. There were thick clots of blood in the toilet. I splashed water on Olivia's face. She stirred but did not wake up.

I called 911.

I tried to pick Olivia up. I turned her on her stomach and she vomited.

Ella screamed.

"It's okay," I said. "She'll be okay…"

Olivia's mother showed up. Ella had called her too. She took a look around and figured it out.

She said, "Not again."

The paramedics arrived. They pumped Olivia's stomach out and took her to the hospital. Then the cops arrived and took a report, first from Ella, and then me.

"I think you should go now," Olivia's mother said to me when the police were gone. "I'll clean up what's left of the miscarriage."

"To the hospital? I'll go there."

"No," she said.

"Where am I supposed to go?"

"Away," she said. "Haven't you done enough damage?"

I walked away from Olivia's home and I walked and walked and walked. I walked for miles. I walked until my feet felt like they were going to fall off and I walked even more, trying to find my dead child so I could hold him or her and say, "It's okay."

XVIII.

I met Olivia's mother for lunch at a café near her office. We sat outside. We sat at a table with a big umbrella, providing shade from the hot sun.

"I'm grateful you agreed to meet me," she said.

"Why would I say no?"

"The way I've treated you, the things I've said to you," she said. "I wouldn't blame you if…"

"I'm here," I said.

"You're here," she said. "Good. Order anything you want. My treat."

"I'm afraid I don't have much of an appetite," I said.

"Well, I'm absolutely famished," she said.

148

She ordered a chicken Caesar's salad. I order a beer and some mozzarella cheese sticks. I wasn't hungry but I knew she would bug me to get something. I didn't care that it was noon and I was drinking a beer in front of her.

"I'm a difficult woman," she said. "I judge too easily, too harshly."

"Is that what you wanted to tell me?"

She made a face, scrunched her nose.

"This whole thing has been a nightmare. The state taking Ella away. Keeping Olivia for observation."

"Yes," I said. Because Ella had found her mother, Child Protective Services took Ella and put her in a foster home because they couldn't reach her father, and they wanted a shrink to determine if she was psychologically damaged. Her father finally took custody of her, but he gave her to Olivia's mother to tend to.

"Paul," she said, "why haven't you gone to see her?"

"I can't."

"She thinks you hate her."

"I don't."

"She thinks you don't love her anymore."

"I've always loved her. But it's too hard."

"Because she blames you?"

"Well, yeah, in part," I said.

Olivia did blame me for the miscarriage, and for trying to kill herself.

"It's all your fucking fault," she said, and hit me in the eye with her fist.

"She had misplaced anger, misplaced blame. That's natural. But there is no one to blame, except God if you believe in God but I never believed there was a God out there. Why would God take babies away like that? She doesn't blame you, Paul, and she needs you and I need you to go see her."

"Thought you'd be happy to see me out of the picture."

"Why do you…say that?"

"You don't like me."

"That is not a fair statement."

"What would be fair?"

"I know you are a kind, decent man," she said, "even if you write some odd plays and poetry."

"Let's leave that out."

"I only want the best for my daughter; and my granddaughter."

"Have you ever realized that your expectations are unrealistic?" I said. "That your demands are the root of Olivia's problems? She's never been able to satisfy you, to get your total approval. Even when things are good, you find fault."

"She needs you."

"I'm in pain," I said.

"So is she. This is why you both must heal."

"And?"

"And I would like you to become Ella's guardian, her legal guardian, in case…"

"In case?"

"Olivia does this again," she said. "I don't want that bastard ex-husband to ever have full custody. He'd never take it. I don't want her to ever spend another hour in some damn foster home."

"You can be her guardian."

"If she tries to commit suicide again, if she is successful the next time, I will die. I will have a heart attack. I almost did this time and I almost did the last time. I won't survive another suicide attempt. If my baby dies, I will die, so I need you to go to her and I need you both to heal. This can be fixed."

I gave this some thought.

"What do I need to do, to be Ella's guardian?"

"Some paperwork, a quick trip to court."

"I'll do that," I said.

"Or…"

"Or?"

"You can marry Olivia, and you'll automatically be Ella's father."

"I can do that," I said.

"Isn't it something, dear?" she said. "I'm asking you to marry my child."

"If I have your permission," I said. I was being facetious, of course.

"Indeed you do…dear." She smiled.

"Thank you," I said.

"Will you go to her?" she asked.

"Yes."

"When?"

"Soon."

"Now?"

"I can go now."

"Please go now, please," she said, and I did.

XIX.

Olivia was in bed. Ella let me into the house. I bent down and hugged her. "I'm happy to see you," I said.

"My mom will be glad you're here," she said.

I walked into the bedroom. Olivia was lying on her side, facing the wall, a blanket cover her body.

"Hey," I said. "Awake?"

"Yeah."

"Can I come in?"

"Don't ask stupid questions." She turned. "My mother called and said you were on the way."

"The woman always ruins a good surprise."

She sat up. "She means well, you know."

"In her way, yes."

She smiled. "I'm glad you're here."

We looked at each other for a bit.

"Come here," she said. "Are you afraid of me?"

"Don't ask stupid questions," I said.

I placed my body next to hers. There we were; two bodies.

"I'm sorry," she said.

"Don't be," I said.

"It wasn't right."

"It's okay."

"It's not okay," she said.

"I'm sorry," she said.

I said, "Accepted."

Her eyes were wet. "I wanted that baby so bad. So much."

"Me too," I said.

My eyes were wet.

"We can try again."

"We can," I said.

"Would you like that?"

"Yes."

"Will you hold me?"

"Yes."

We held each other for a long time. We fell asleep that way. We shared dreams.

The next day we both went to an Alcoholics Anonymous meeting.

XX.

I picked up the newspaper one morning and saw something that made my heart skip a beat.

I sat there, sipping coffee as Olivia made breakfast and Ella was reading a book; she was getting ready for school and I was getting ready for work and Olivia was getting us both ready. It was a regular scene of domestic bliss.

I read this headline: **Local Man's Body Found in Own Backyard.**

And the black and white photo was Jeff.

Sub-headline: **"Missing for over two years," says wife, arrested for murder**.

Caption under photo: *Jeffrey Wayne Bonfils, reported missing by his wife, Lisa Patrice Bonfils, was found buried in the backyard of his house.*

Coffee flew out of my nostrils.

"Gross," Ella said.

"You okay?" Olivia asked.

"Yeah," I said.

I went to work (backbreaking construction labor—it paid better than any job I've ever had) and thought about Jeff all day. I was obsessed. I showed the paper to everyone on the job site and said, "You hear about this shit?"

Most had not.

Some said, "Yeah. It's always the wife or husband, eh?"

"Usually the wife," said someone else, "those crazy killing bitches."

At home, I watched the local news on TV. There was a story. "Wife Lisa Bonfils has confessed to the crime," said the anchorman, "saying she killed her husband in a moment of anger when he failed to come home one night. She believed he was having an affair. She buried the body in their backyard, hid his car in the garage, and filed a missing person's report."

I thought of the day I drove over to talk to her. I thought of all the wondering and worrying since. She had asked me to help her. She had acted like she didn't know where Jeff was.

What if she had killed me too? What if I had told her he was out drinking with me?

I imagined my body buried next to his.

I thought of all the things I would never had to go through the past two years if Lisa Bonfils had murdered me.

I decided I was happy to be alive.

I wondered, too, if his death was my fault. Had I not gone to the grocery store, had I not been sitting in my car, smoking and drinking, had I not gone to the bar with him, had I not let him keep buying beer...

Had I not stolen his food.

Was I ashamed? We are all ashamed of our pasts.

I decided I had to live in the now.

Day by day, as the Program said.

***

I got into bed with Olivia. She was reading a paperback romance. I put my head on her five-month pregnant belly.

She ran her fingers through my hair.

"When will he start kicking?" I asked.

For some reason, we both knew the fetus was a boy. In our heart of hearts, we just knew.

"Soon," my wife said, "soon."

XXI.

I had a job and Olivia didn't.

And that was okay. She was seven months and she couldn't stand on her feet all day at the grocery store. We had to pinch pennies, but I was making enough for the family. I was the breadwinner.

Construction work is tricky work. You don't need a degree in anything to figure out manual labor, so the brightest guys didn't surround me. It wasn't steady work; you could go a week or two without a job. That's why it paid well. Fortunately, there was a housing boom in Santa Cruz and there was ample work going around.

I was on one job site with a bunch of guys ten years younger than me - all in great shape, walking around the job with their shirts off, showing tanned, trim muscle. Women liked to walk by and look, and the guys liked to whistle at the women and show off their virile stuff. All these kids cared about was a paycheck, booze, and pussy.

They called me 'pops.' I liked to think this wasn't because I was ten years older, but for the fact that I had a baby coming.

"Hey, pops!" they said one day after work, a Friday. "We're all going to this titty bar. Come along."

"I can't," I said.

"Don't be such a fuddy-duddy, pops," they said.

"One, I don't drink anymore," I said, "and two, I have a pregnant wife and daughter to get home to."

"Pregnant daughter too?"

Laughter.

These guys.

"Hey, friend of Bill, we won't tell Bill," they said.

"One hour, pops," they said, "you can drink a soda-pop and see what you've been missing."

"Oh," I said, "I've had enough, I'm not missing anything."

Driving home, a Mercedez-Benz, going eighty-miles-an-hour, ran a red light and slammed into my car.

My last thought: My family.

No, my last thought was: I should have gone to the titty bar.

And I thought of Jeff, and how anything could happen in this goddamn life.

***

Olivia, round and plump, was sitting by my side when I woke up in the hospital.

"Thank God, Paul," she said.

"What happened?" It hurt to talk.

"There was an accident," she said.

I remembered. And then there was pain. So much pain, all through my body. I couldn't feel my right arm and knew I had probably lost it. No, it was still there, but in a cast. My face was bandaged up from flying glass that had cut into my flesh. The doctor would later tell me I lost an eye, my left eye. My ribs were bruised and my body had lacerations.

"When the police called," she said.

"What?"

"I thought I was going to have another miscarriage because I thought you were dead."

I felt a dreadful panic mixed with my pain.

"The baby?"

She touched her belly.

"Still in there."

"Oh," I said, "oh."

"Does it hurt?

"I know the true meaning of agony," I said.

She rang for the nurse, and then came the doctor, and then came the news. I survived the accident, and all I lost was an eye.

"It could have been worse," said the doctor.

***

The teenage kid was driving his parents' car; he came from a rich family. He was drunk and he didn't have a license. The family's insurance company offered a very generous settlement - enough for me to take several years off from work, tend to my family, even afford another baby if we wanted.

Enough to keep me in a good supply of stylish glass eyes.

I wanted to wear an eye patch. I thought that would be sexy. Olivia hated it. She could live with a glass eye.

Looking at the world with one eye was to see it differently.

XXII.

I woke up and the bed was wet. Sticky fluid soaked the sheets under me.

"Water broke," Olivia said, "it's time."

I helped her out of bed and into a robe.

I called a taxi and woke Ella.

"It's time," I said to Ella.

"My baby brother is coming?" She was excited.

"It's time!"

We danced around.

"What the hell are you two doing?!" Olivia yelled.

"Taxi is on the way," I said.

"Why are we taking a cab?" Ella asked.

"I'm too afraid to drive," I said.

"Hurry," I told the cab driver.

"She's not going to have it in my car, is she?"

"I might," Olivia said, groaning.

"Well," he said, "it would be the third baby to be born in my ride."

***

If the baby is a girl, I thought, our hearts would have been wrong all this time.

I was in the delivery room, and I saw my son being born. It happened fast, it wasn't a long labor. The still, purple and blue thing came out of her like a fish. The doctor slapped him on the ass and he woke, crying, moving.

"A boy," he said. The umbilical cord was cut and the baby was placed on Olivia's stomach for her to see.

"Oh," my wife said, "oh, there he is. I've known him forever, for many lives, across the stars, across the galaxies, and he is with me now…"

Then came the afterbirth, the placenta. I was told about it but I wasn't expecting it to look like something from outer space.

***

Ella and I visited our wife and mother and new baby. We took turns holding the child.

"Get used to it," I said to Ella, "you're going to be doing a lot of babysitting."

"I want one of these, some day," Ella said, fascinated with her baby brother.

"Not for another ten years," Olivia said, "or even more."

I held my son and looked at his sleeping face with my one eye and thought yes, anything could happen, and I was happy to be alive.

***

Ella and I left the hospital to go get ice cream across the street. It was a good time for some sweet, cold ice cream cones.

The sun was peeking through the clouds. Rays of light shone down on the earth.

Rays.

I smiled, and then I laughed.

"What is it?" Ella asked.

"Nothing," I said.

I could have died right then and there and I would have gone to Heaven the happiest man on the planet.

What Happens Between Literary Agents and Clients

You're at this party in Tribeca and you really don't want to be there, but there you are. What you hate about the evening: very little, if any, business calls. You keep checking your cell to make sure it's getting reception. You strike up a conversation with a young woman with long brown hair; you really like her eyes. She touches you, you touch her back; you play with her long hair, twist it in your fingers, smell her perfume and tell her you approve. The next thing you know you're in one of the bedrooms having sex on a pile of coats. When the hasty act is done, you leave the room first. No one at the party seems to notice your indiscretion; you stop feeling guilty and begin to feel like a Norseman who has just ravaged a princess on the high seas of a badly written Viking romance novel. You get yourself a new drink, and you *need* a drink; you go out to the balcony and sit down. Two minutes later, the young woman joins you. She also has a cocktail and she appears freshly fucked - glowing and smiling.

"So," you say.

"So," she says.

"That was something else," you say.

"Oh yeah," she laughs. "Do you do this sort of thing often?"

"No," you lie.

"Me either," she goes.

You ask her name.

"Trinity."

"That's really your name?"

"Like *The Matrix* movies," she says.

You nod and say, "I like it."

"That's my chat room handle anyway," she says. "Do you do the Internet?"

"Only e-mail."

"And porn?"

You smile and say, "Who doesn't look at porn on the Net?"

"My husband, he looks at it all the time."

"Your husband?"

"Jacks off to the weirdest sites."

"Husband."

"You know my husband, right? I saw you talking to him like you were old friends. William Blount."

"Holy shit," you say, "you're Bill Blount's *wife?*"

"Relax," Trinity says. "He has no idea what we just did. He never notices anything. Terrorists could fly a plane into the building down the street and he wouldn't take heed. It's okay."

"I didn't know you were married."

"I didn't tell you," she says, "Does it matter?"

You're like, "No."

"Ever do cybersex?" she asks.

"Once or twice."

"I do it all the time," she says. "It's fun. I like it."

"Good for you."

"So what do you do? And what's your name?"

You tell her your name, and tell her what you do for a living. She says, "An agent? Like, you represent *actors?*"

"Writers."

"What?"

"Novels and screenplays," you say.

Under thirty, you're the youngest and hottest mover of product at a big and well-known agency. You know how to find the stars in the piles of manuscripts. You don't say this to Trinity.

"Oh," she says.

"Your husband publishes writers," you say.

"Oh," Trinity says, "I never talk to him about his work. Have you always been an agent?"

"I used to deliver pizzas when I was a kid," you say. "I was a bike messenger in college. Then I tried my hand as a junior stockbroker."

"Stocks! I love playing the stocks. I have an Ameritrade account," she says.

"Yeah?"

"I am a daytrader."

You tell her you do a little daytrading on your Schwab account.

"Sometimes I make money, sometimes I don't," she says. "Usually I do. What I like most, daytrading and having cybersex at the same time."

"Sounds like fun."

"So why aren't you on Wall Street anymore?"

"Stress," you say.

"There's no stress being an agent?"

"It's a different kind."

"As long as you're happy. Are you happy?"

You have to think about that.

You say, "Yes."

You say, "Yes, I am."

"That's good; it's good to be happy. That's all that matters, right?"

"Right."

She says, "So, who are your hot clients?"

"Right now I have two."

You're more than happy to talk about this.

"They're different as different can be. One is this wild fellow from Arkansas; he wrote a novel called *Sunlight Reflections on a Crushed Beer Can*. It's the ultimate tome on white trailer park trash. It's an unbearably sad work of bone-crushing genius - a 980-page monster of a book."

Trinity says, "980 pages?!"

She goes, "I'll wait for the movie."

"There very well may be a movie," you tell her; "I'm talking to several producers. Now, my *other* precocity has written a collection of eight stories, a slim but dynamic volume, called *Sex, Drugs, General Mayhem and Death in Junior High*. The writer, by the way, is a thirteen-year-old girl."

"Junior high is the worst," Trinity says, "kids can be truly evil in those awkward years."

"Yes, that's what my young author claims."

"Uh-oh," Trinity says, "William is looking at us."

"He is?"

"It's okay. I better go to him."

"Okay."

"It was fun."

"Yeah."

She leaves. You remain on the balcony. Your cell rings. The caller sounds far away. He's a publisher you know in Osaka.

"Takayuki-san," you say. "How goes it?"

"Let us talk dinero," Takayuki says.

He wants to buy the Japanese rights to four books you rep. You're ready to make a deal tonight; doing so makes you feel complete when you finally go to bed. You'll wake up feeling *right*.

***

The next day. Noon. Interior: at the office. You get a phone call from Los Angeles; it's Bernard Goldman, a producer, and he's distraught.

"Your client, man," Bernard says, "your client, Johnny Ray Thorn…"

"What about him?"

"thought it was all an act, a ruse, you didn't tell me he was an *actual fucking hick!*"

164

"He wrote a novel about hicks," you say. "What did you think?"

"But, yeah," Bernard says, "I didn't know he *was* one!"

"What happened?"

"I invited him to this party in Bel Air. Belairbelairbelair, and who do I allow to enter the gates of the Elysian hills? I guess I should have checked him out first, but man oh man you could've given me some kind of heads up here, guy. He comes to the fucking party in smelly old overalls and no shoes! All three hundred and twenty-five pounds of him! And he proceeds to get drunk as a skunk and grab-asses every starlet in the vicinity. Mind you, some of these girls didn't mind, they found him kind of amusing, but it was as embarrassing as walking into green light meeting without my prize Rolex. I mean, really, guy! I mean, I love *Sunlight Reflections on a Crushed Beer Can* and I want to get the abridged version up on the celluloid, but I do *not* want this hillbilly mofo on the set. I mean, he's talking like he's going to be at every shoot and have say-so on all the dailies, but I declare this here and now, dude: it ain't gonna happen. No way, no how."

"Bernard," you say sincerely, "I don't know what to tell you; I'm sorry the meet didn't go well."

"The guy can tell a story on paper, but he should be locked away for the good of all humanity."

"Nevertheless," you say, "the movie's going to be a hit."

"Let's hope so. After all, I'm *banking* on it."

"So let's sign on it."

"I can't yet. You know how it goes."

You always know how it goes.

An hour later, Johnny Ray Thorn calls from his hotel room in Century City.

"This place is weird," he says, "and the people are weird."

"Maybe it's time to go home, Johnny Ray, Arkansas is calling. Eh?"

165

"Arkansas can kiss my hairy ass," says Johnny Ray. "I booked a flight to New York. I'm leaving in two hours."

"New York?" you say, rubbing your forehead very hard. "Why New York?"

"Maybe I can do some book signings. I talked to the lady in publicity. She says she can set something up in a day or two. My novel is still selling, right?"

"Flying off the shelves," you say. "Flying."

"So no problem. I'm flying too."

"Well," you say, "call me when you get in."

"Isn't that little girl in New York?" Johnny Ray asks. "You represent her? The schoolgirl slut?"

You hesitate and then say, "Molli Runes. She is here doing promo stuff."

"Yeah, that's what I read. I'd like to meet her."

"She's very busy, you know."

"I wanna meet her."

***

Molli Runes is at the SoHo Grand in a $600-a-day room. She has a reading and signing at six, another reading at nine, and two talk shows in the morning. Her story collection is #5 on The List, she's going to be in *The Village Voice's* "Writers on the Verge" Issue, and you hear rumors she may be up for a PEN/Hemingway Award. Or was that the Faulkner? You can never get the two straight. Does it matter? Either way, that's sales and attention and you've been telling her to get to work on that novel; like any teenage girl, she's stubborn to listen.

You go to see her at the SoHo to escort her to the events; you are *not* prepared for a naked and apparently young author bouncing up and down on the bed. She has a crack pipe in one hand, a lighter in the other. Her hair is sticking out in all directions.

Her body is pale pink, her pubic hair wispy and her breasts like tiny apples (so they say).

"Hey!" she goes. "There you are!"

"Oh hell," you mutter. "Molli, please put some clothes on."

You look at the wall.

"I know you're not such a *prude.*"

"Get dressed."

"What do you have against the human body?" She hops off the bed and she's next to you, looking up at your closed eyes. She smells like hotel soap and rock cocaine.

"Molli."

"Will you look at me?"

You look at her.

"Why don't you get naked," she says.

"Why don't you get dressed."

"Why don't we *fuck.* I need to get royally fucked. I've been smoking this bad shit for an hour and I'm horny as a horny toad."

She giggles. You are *not* Humbert Humbert; still, you cannot help yourself from looking. You fear she will destroy many men when she's ten years older, if she hasn't destroyed them already. In her short fiction, the "I" has slept with teachers and older men who live across the street and give the "I" marijuana and tequila.

"Where is your mother?"

"She's not here."

"Where did she go?"

"She didn't come. She's back at home, fucking her new boyfriend."

"She let you travel *alone?*"

"I'm a big girl," Molli says and looks at her breasts. "Well, maybe I'm *not* big, but I can travel to The Big Ol' Apple by myself. They gave me this room. I have my own credit card, thanks to you."

"Yeah?"

"Thanks to *you,* I'm semi-rich."

"Yes, Molli," you say, "and with such things - there is a certain amount of responsibility."

"Poo on that. Let's celebrate my impending fame." She tugs at your arm and says, "Let's have a sticky quickie. Don't worry, I'll never let a biographer in on this special moment."

All you can do is envision the repercussions. She reminds you of the James Bond movie *For Your Eyes Only*, and the scene where a blonde underage nympho ice skater tries to entice Roger Moore into bed with her pink naked body; but Bond says, "Don't grow up too fast," and turns her down. When you saw the movie, you thought: *Oh, Mr. Bond!*

You take Molli's crack pipe away.

"Hey!"

"There's a book to promote."

"Bummer."

You say, "This is your career."

"You have a point. It's all that matters, right?"

"Right."

***

Molli does the Catholic schoolgirl routine: plaid skirt, white blouse, black penny loafers, off-white knee-high socks. She knows what she's doing and you know she'll get far and for the duration (another collection, a novel, maybe a movie, then oblivion) you will get fifteen percent.

At the six o'clock bookstore gig, she performs well. She reads two stories from her book, thirty minutes total, and you're amazed at her delivery: the projection, the dramatic pauses, the levels in her voice, the different voices she gives to her characters. She must have had some training in drama or speech. You see about thirty people at the store and everyone buys books. A young man from the publisher's publicity department is present. He says he has a limo to whisk Molli to her next gig.

"A limo," Molli says. "Coolness."

The limo has a fully stocked bar. Molli makes herself a vodka tonic; you know it's pointless to admonish her. You make yourself a Tom Collins, drink it fast, and make another.

"Better watch it," Molli says, "you'll get drunk."

"I never get drunk," you say and this is true. You can drink and drink, and the best you can do is a damn fine buzz. You have never been shit-faced in your life.

"My whole family. Alcoholics. Especially my Mom. Sometimes I think I shouldn't drink."

"You should not. You're too young."

She laughs and says in a snotty high-pitched tone, "And I'm too young to have published a book full of sex and debauchery."

She has a point.

She gives you her vodka tonic.

"You finish it. I have another reading to do."

You drink her drink.

At the second reading, the one person you don't expect to see is there; you're hoping you wouldn't see him. Johnny Ray Thorn, all six-foot-five, three hundred-plus pounds of him. He's impressive: barrel-chest, big belly, thick arms. His legs are very skinny. His hair is unwashed, and he's missing three front teeth. What did the L.A. Times say about his author photo? The most unattractive and scary-looking Southern writer since Harry Crews. That's Johnny Ray Thorn, all right, and damn it all if you're not proud of the sonofabitch; you're just not prepared for him being here, *here*. At least he's wearing shoes. He's wearing the overalls; he's told you it's the only clothes he feels comfortable in. There are fifty, sixty people at this reading, and every one of them looks at Johnny Ray with the appropriate literary snobbish glance, one you've seen all too often, as if to say, "What is that trash doing

169

here?" But a young fellow wearing a brown sports coat and horn-rimmed glasses says, "Aren't you John Thorn? You wrote that trailer park novel, right?"

"Yeah," Johnny Ray says flatly, "that be me."

"I loved your book."

"Thank you kindly."

"Johnny," you say. "Jonathan."

"I love it when you call me that."

"You made it."

"It was a hairy flight," he says. "Hairy like a skunk's ass, and just as smelly. Lots of bumps in the air. What do they call that stuff? Turby. But I had this." He removes a flask from his overalls. "Always helps."

"And what's that?" Molli says.

"Moonshine, baby," says Johnny Ray. "Distilled it myself. My grandpapppy's original recipe."

"Wow."

"You're Miss Runes."

"And you're Mr. Thorn."

"Seems we have much in common."

"Yeah, our names pop up on the same bestseller lists."

"And we have this crazy man."

Johnny Ray wraps a big arm around your neck. You wince. You smile. You can smell his armpit. Molli slaps you on the ass. They both laugh.

"Well," you say.

"I read your stories," Johnny Ray says letting you go and stepping toward Molli, "and I wanted to meet you."

Molli stares up at him like she would view a mountain in the desert.

"I can't say I've read yours. I have it, but it's just too big for a girl like me."

"One day you'll be able to take it."

"I'm sure I will."

"Enough of this," you say. "Let's get out of here."

"Yeah," Molli says, "we have a stretch."

**

There are five of you in the limo. Molly and Johny Ray invited the fellow in the brown jacket and a skinny clerk from the bookstore; they are both aspiring writers and they want to show you their stuff, they want book deals, they want to be famous. They are like nineteen-year-old porn actresses who've shot two videos with visions of money and underground fame. You usually tell them (on the phone) that you have too many clients, but since they're here in the limo and drinking martinis, you tell them, "Send me what you have, here's my card, send me your novel or story collection, let's see what you got."

The bookstore clerk says she has an historical novel she's been working on since she was Molli's age; the fellow in the jacket says he's written "the new novel."

"And what's that?" Johnny Ray says. "What's that shit?"

"My novel would blow you away, man."

"It would have to be a mighty wind," Molli says, "to blow such a big guy like Johnny Ray away."

Something happens - tires screech, brakes groan, there's a thump and a smash and everyone spills their drinks on themselves. Molli yelps. The limousine has come to a stop. Seems another limousine - a longer one - has hit yours. The longer limo overflows with drunken prep school boys in blue jackets and red ties. They all have blonde hair.

Other cars honk. Cabs, mostly. The two limo drivers yell at each other in the street.

"What the fuck?" the prep school boys say. "Someone's gonna pay for screwing up our night."

Molli opens the sun roof and pops her head out.

"What's with you jackasses? Can't you hire a driver who can *drive?*"

"Hey, look at the little girl."

Molli sticks out her tongue. She opens her white blouse and flashes her tits. She giggles and ducks back in the limo. The boys—half a dozen of them—surround the limo, pound on the windows; they say they want Molli to come out.

"Step out, honey," they say, "we wanna rape you!"

"Hold this," Johnny Ray says, handing you his flask. He walks out of the limo like Godzilla emerging from the ocean. The boys all go quiet.

Your star author defends the honor of your other star author by beating the living crap out of the preppies; you sniff the flask. Smells like gasoline; the moonshine burns your throat but it gives you an immediate buzz, the best you've ever had. So you drink more.

***

You wake up on a bed in the SoHo Grand. It's six a.m. Molli is next to you and she's getting up. She's wearing pink pajamas. Johnny Ray is asleep on the floor. Your head is pounding and your eyes hurt. It's your first hangover.

"Oh God," you say.

"Don't worry, nothing happened," Molli says. "I have to get a shower. Morning talk show, remember? Go back to sleep."

You close your eyes. You open your eyes three hours later. Johnny Ray is talking on your cell phone. You sit up.

"He's awake," Johnny Ray says. He holds out the phone. "It's for you. Good news."

"Who is it?"

"L.A."

It's Bernard Goldman.

"Hey, guy," he says. "Okay, so Thorn ain't so bad. It's all in the presentation, but the man has talent. Let's seal the deal."

You do some talking; say "FedEx the paperwork to my office," and you go to the bathroom and piss. You almost puke. Walls are still spinning. You don't like this feeling.

Johnny Ray is sitting on the bed and looking out the window.

"They're really gonna make a movie of my life," he says. "Weird."

"Where's Molli?"

"She took off to her TV thing. I wanna do TV things."

"What happened last night?"

"Let's see. We got in a fender bender, I whooped some Central Park rich ass that needed a whooping, we escaped the cops, and you got drunk as a skunk, my friend."

"You didn't do anything with Molli, did you?"

"Oh, man, that's a dumb thing to ask."

"Did I?"

"We had to carry you up here."

"I've never been drunk," you say.

"Welcome to the real world."

"Drunk people do dumb things."

"Look, about Molli," he says. "She's a child. This whole wayward slut thing is an act. We talked; she's a virgin. She knows the game. It sells books, right?"

"Right."

"And that's all that matters, right?"

"Right."

"So why don't you get washed up and let's go get us some pancakes?" he says. "Do you like pancakes?"

"Jonathan," you say, "right now I could eat a whole stack of them. Lots of butter, lots of syrup."

173

"Breakfast is a very, very important thing in a man's life."
You couldn't agree more.

AND THEN IT HAPPENED

Then a moment passed and all was changed.
- Samuel Beckett

I come from a dizzy land where the lottery is the basis for reality.
- Jorge Luis Borges

Harry M. Evans won the California State Lottery three days after turning thirty-three. There hadn't been a winner for several weeks and the jackpot was $88 million. He heard the winning numbers on the radio while driving away from his ex-wife's house. It used to be his home. He had been visiting Isabelle, his eight-year-old daughter; he heard the numbers and looked at his lottery ticket and saw the same exact numbers and then crashed his ten-year-old Mustang convertible into a thick and bent oak tree.

He stumbled away from the unfortunate wreck, bleeding at the head and mouth, clutching his winning ticket like a Knights Templar who'd just found the Holy Grail.

He walked twelve blocks toward downtown and stopped at a twenty-four-hour Kinko's, where he photocopied the ticket.

The pink-haired young woman working behind the counter had blue eyes and bright white teeth and small pink lips.

She said, "You're bleeding, sir."

"I know."

"Are you all right?"

"I'm just fine. Thank you for asking."

They smiled at each other and he paid the eight cents for his photocopy.

The pink-haired young woman with the blue eyes and the bright white teeth and small pink lips handed him some tissues and said, "Here. Take these."

"Thanks again."

"You sure you're all right?" she asked. She seemed genuinely concerned. He liked that. Her name tag read **"DENISE."**

"I've never been better, Denise," said Harry M. Evans.

He flagged a taxicab and went home. The ride cost $11 plus a $2 tip; this was a good thing because his wallet contained only a $10 bill and five ones. He was bored with being consistently broke. He stared at the photocopy of the ticket for about an hour and decided it couldn't be the real deal. He called the California Lottery Commission's automated line; a recording read off the same numbers.

He verified this when the 11:00 news showed the evening's winning numbers.

In bed he stared at his numbers. Then it was four in the morning. He didn't think he'd sleep but he did; he dreamt about the numbers dancing around, running away from him, taunting him. He called in sick to work.

"I ate something bad, my stomach is turning inside out."

"You've missed too many days," the general manager at the department store said. "I've warned you more than once, *Evans.*"

Harry was a retail worker at the Shopping Mall, selling men's clothes and cologne and kissing a lot of ass on the sales floor to get that minimum wage plus 13% commission.

He hated the job.

So he said, "Fire me."

He said, "I don't care."

He said, "Do it."

The GM said, "Fire you? So you can collect unemployment on our dime? Think again, *Evans.*"

"Then I quit."

"You what? What say you?"

"I quit," Harry said.

"Good," his ex-boss said and hung up.

Harry said to himself: "Well that's that." He started to feel insecure about the future of things, et cetera.

On the morning news showed the winning numbers again and an anchor said: "The $88 million ticket was sold right here, at a small liquor store…"

He called an escort service out of the Yellow Pages. Why? The loneliness of his good fortune was unbearable; he was excited and full of adrenaline.

It was 10 a.m.

"Do you send girls out this early?"

"Twenty-four-seven, honey," the woman on the other line said, and then she blew her breath into the phone.

"I want the best you got."

"We got the best in town, baby," and then she coughed and the cough sounded painful. "Sorry. What can we do for you?"

"I want a blonde," he said.

"We have plenty of *those.*"

He gave his MasterCard number. He had about $600 of available credit. An hour later, a young woman with a blonde wig showed up. He didn't mind the wig. She wore a green mini-skirt and a white blouse.

"What do you want to do?"

"Everything."

"Everything could be too much."

"Are you kidding?"

"I never joke, guy."

"So what can I get?"

"What do you want?"

"I want a lot."

"It'll cost you."

"That's all right."

When she left, he felt lonelier and there wasn't much of a balance left on his card. Later, he called his ex-wife and asked to speak to his daughter.

"What do you want to talk to her about?"

"That's none of your business."

"I'm her mother, and it is my business."

"Let's not do this," he said, "not right now."

Joanna sighed the sigh of a disgruntled mother.

Harry said, "I just want to hear her voice."

Joanna sighed again.

"Daddy," said Isabelle.

"Oh," Harry said, "I just want you to know, I love you very much."

"Oh," she said, "I love you too, Daddy."

*"*And I want you to know real soon the world will be yours."

"Okay."

The next call was to the Lottery Commission. He had to go through several menus to get a live voice on the other line. He said he was the winner and no one seemed impressed and was transferred three times until he was, apparently, connected to the right person.

A man on the other line said, "Can you prove this?"

He had a very deep voice, like the actor James Earl Jones.

"I hope I can," Harry said.

"Send me a fax of the ticket."

"I can do that."

"Here's my fax number..."

Harry had a large, clunky fax machine in his closet - a Christmas gift from his father and stepmother. It was still in the box, sealed. He got the machine out of the box, read the instructions, and hooked it to his phone line. He faxed the photocopy to the man with the deep voice at the Lottery Commission.

The man with the deep voice called back within five minutes and said, "Looks like this is it. We can come down to San Diego immediately and begin the process."

Harry had to take sleeping pills that night because, after all, he was too excited to relax.

***

People began to call when the news got out.

First, of course: Joanna. "Is this for real? I mean..."

"Yes," he said. He wondered if that check from the State would actually clear. He'd opted for the straight payout, instead of twenty annual checks; after taxes, it came to about $38 million.

"So," said his ex-wife, "I've been thinking about this."

"I bet you have," he said.

"What's my cut?"

He closed his eyes.

"What do I get?"

"You don't get shit," he told her; he hated that it sounded good to utter those words.

"What was that?"

"You heard me."

"I get a cut," Joanna said, her voice close to shouting, "I get *something.*"

"Hey," Harry said, "did you forget you're no longer my wife? You have not been my wife for a long, long time."

"We have a *goddamn child,*" Joanna said. "You know?"

"Yeah," he said. "I know."

"What about *her?*"

"I'll take care of her."

"And what about *me?*"

"You," he said happily, "can go fuck yourself."

He didn't want to be this way; this wasn't him.

"You don't have to be so crude," Joanna said.

"Hey," he said, "I'm sorry."

She said, "Asshole."

He listened to her breathing.

"You can't *do* this."

"Oh...yes I can."

"It's not right. I'll sue you."

"Yeah," Harry said.

"You're going to be sorry, you know that," she said. "You're going to be *sorry.*"

"Yeah," he said. "I know."

"I hate you."

"Yes," he said. "I know."

"So will Isabelle," she said, "I'll make sure of that."

And she hung up.

***

"Harrison," said his stepmother, Alexia, long distance, "Harrison Marvin Evans, can you *hear* me, kiddo?"

"I hear you, Mom."

He never liked being called Harrison and she knew this; she did it just to annoy him.

"Is this a good connection?" she asked.

"It is, Mom."

He never liked calling her Mom, but she had always insisted. So did his father, who married her when Harry was ten years old.

"I hear static, Harrison."

"You're coming in fine."

She was calling from Sacramento.

"Is that you they're talking about on the news?"

"I believe it is," said Harry. "What are they saying?"

"That you're 'rich'. Is this true?"

Before he could reply, his father, Gerrold, got on the other line and said, "Harry? Harry, my boy, is it true?"

"Dad," he said, "well—"

"I'm *talk*ing to him," said Alexia.

"Hang up," Gerrold said, *"I'm* talking to him now."

"WELL!" Alexia said and slammed down her phone.

"We can talk safely now," Gerrold said. "So…is it true?"

"Yes."

"Why didn't you call?"

"I meant to. I was about to."

"This is grand news."

"It is; it is. Isn't it? It is."

"I always knew you were destined for great things, son."

"Well…"

"Listen."

"Dad."

"Listen."

"Dad, I am."

"Alexia, your mother, she's already spending your money," and he chuckled but it was a hollow sound over the phone.

"I don't understand," Harry said.

"She has ideas for investments, gifts, things - *things* she wants and has designs on..."

"Um," said Harry.

"Don't let her," Gerrold Evans said, "don't let her talk you into anything stupid and silly."

"I won't."

"And *don't* give her any money, okay?"

"Okay."

"Harry?"

"Dad."

"I'm *serious.*"

"I know."

"I'm serious," he said again. "You don't know how…"

"I understand."

Silence.

"Do you *understand?*" the father asked.

"Yes."

"Good. Now…"

"What should I…"

"Don't take her calls."

"Not at all?"

"Hang up on her if she calls."

"Okay."

"She's going crazy about this, you know," and again that chuckle.

"I see," Harry said.

"She thinks your money is hers…because she helped raise you and all."

"Oh," Harry said.

"If only your real mother could see you now!" said Gerrold.

"Yeah," Harry said. She died when he was five. He didn't remember her. She was a series of photographs from someone else's life. She looked a lot like Isabelle. Isabelle looked a lot like his dead mother.

"She would've been proud," Gerrold said, "rest her beautiful bones."

How could he reply to that? He said, "I would hope so…"

"I," said his father's sincere sixty-year-old voice from the northern region of California, "am proud of you, son. Listen to me, okay?"

"I'm listening."

"Strange people will be looking you up."

"I have a feeling they will."

"Get a lawyer."

"Have one."

"Good, good, I knew I raised you right. Eh?"

Harry laughed.

"It may seem funny now…"

***

First, there were his co-workers, former co-workers.

Bob, a very tall guy with wispy brown hair whom Harry seldom talked to. He called and asked for $650. No hello, no small talk, no how-you-doing. Bob said, "Loan me $650. I'm good for it till pay day."

"Why?"

"Why? *Why?* Why does *any*one need money? I need to pay my rent, you jackass. I'm behind."

"But why are you asking me?"

"What do you *think?* Everyone *knows.* I heard. You're like mega rich."

"I haven't even been paid yet. That takes time."

"What? You don't have the money?"

"Not yet."

"When will you get it?"

"I don't know," Harry lied.

"When you do know, loan me $650."

"Bob."

"Shit, loan me - *give me.* You can afford it. Give me a grand. What's $1,000 to a millionaire?"

"I'll think about it," Harry said.

"Think? What's there to think?"

"I have to go, Bob."

"Go? Go where?"

"There's someone at my door, Bob."

"We'll talk, Harry."

Bob slammed his phone down.

Then the phone rang again. He thought it was Bob but it was Rachel Arnold, a woman from work. She wasn't at work.

"I called in sick," she said, "I'm at home."

She was always calling in sick.

Harry said, "I hope it's not too bad."

"I'm naked in bed."

"Yeah?"

"So I heard," she said. "About, you know."

"Seems everyone has."

"Congrats."

"Thanks."

"So I was thinking about that date you asked me out on," she said.

"Oh yeah," he said. He'd asked her out two months ago. Her reply: "I'll get back to you."

"Yeah," Rachel said; "so maybe it's time we do it. You know - some drinks, dancing. Dinner and movie. What did you have in mind? Where did you want to take me?"

"To bed," Harry said.

"Well, get right to the point why don't you. I never knew you had it in you to be so brazen and aggressive. Why, you *pig* you. You brute, you beast, you cad."

"I was joking."

"No you weren't."

"Actually, I was."

"Take me to dinner," she said. "Somewhere fancy."

"I'll get back to you," he said.

"What?"

"Bye Rachel," he said.

Well, that certainly felt good, thought Harry.

The phone rang. It was Alexia.

"Harrison," she said, "I've been trying to call and your phone has been busy."

"I'm popular today, Mom."

"You should get call waiting. God knows you can afford it now. We need to *talk*, Harrison," said his stepmother. "We need to talk about what we're going to *do* with that money."

He couldn't do what his father had told him; he couldn't just hang up.

"Harrison? Are you there?"

"I am."

"Did you hear what I said, kiddo?"

"Once I get it," he said.

"Yes, once you get it. First, don't take the annual payments. Cash out for the lump sum. It's the smart thing to do."

He didn't tell her he'd done that already.

"Second," she said, "I have some investment ideas."

"Mom," he said, "someone's at the door."

"I beg your pardon?"

"I need to answer the door."

"Tell them to go away; tell them you're busy."

"I have to get it. I'll talk to you later."

"Harrison."

"I have to go."

"HARRISON MARVIN EVANS!"

He hung up. The phone rang. He decided not to get it. The answering machine – an old and clunky device he'd had for twelve years – picked it up.

It was Joanna.

"Harry," she said, "I need to talk to you. Call me ASAP."

The phone rang again. He let the answering machine pick it up again.

"Harrison," Alexia's voice said, "did you get rid of whomever is at the damn door? Well, when you do, call me. *We need* to seriously talk about our money."

The phone rang.

On the answering machine: "Hey, Harry! It's your old cousin Pete! Long time no talk. And I would like to talk. You got my number, right? Here it is again…"

He hadn't talked to or seen Pete in years.

The phone rang. On the answering machine: "Mr. Evans, this is Prescott Daniels from the California Lottery Commission---"

He picked up the phone.

"Yes," he said, "I'm here."

"Ah, Mr. Evans. Congratulations."

"Thank you."

"I'm sure you've been hearing that quite a bit…and will continue to do so. Now, I would like to inform you that the money shall be transferred into your account within seven-to-ten business days. These things take time, I'm afraid. We *are* the government, after all…"

***

He needed cold hard cash. He had a final paycheck coming. He wanted to have it mailed but he was broke and needed the money immediately. So he went to that big ugly department store. His former co-workers stared at him, whispered, pointed. Maybe he wanted to gloat - he didn't feel bad at all. He walked straight to the back of the store. The GM was sitting behind a small metal desk, wearing a white dress shirt, cheap tie; he had a stain of mustard on his chin. The guy was tall and thin and in his mid-twenties; he looked up and said, "What are *you* doing here? Don't bother begging for your job back, Evans."

"I came for my last check," Harry said.

"Yeah yeah yeah, that's what I figured," said the GM, opening a drawer, reaching in, and handing over an envelope.

On the envelope was scrawled, in big block letters: **EVANS**

"Thank you," Harry said and turned to leave.

"Think you're something special now, don't you?" said the GM. "Well, you're not. You hear me? You're not! You're a slacker who never takes anything seriously and a year from now you'll be back begging for your job and I'll laugh at you and turn you away!"

Harry stopped.

"What do you have to say to *that*, Mr. Big Shot Lottery Winner? Huh? Tell me, Mr. *Special.*"

Harry walked away from what promised to be a bad scene. As much as he'd like to punch the GM in the mouth or kick the guy in the balls, it would only cause him trouble and he wanted to be done with the place.

He immediately encountered Bob, who was wearing a thin tie. Bob's new goatee sprouted from his chin like a dark fungus.

"What the fuck, Harry," said Bob, hitting Harry's chest with an open palm.

"Hey," said Harry.

"What's $1000 to you, man?" and Bob hit Harry again, but not hard. The GM was watching and didn't make a move to stop it.

"I don't have $1000," Harry said.

"Yeah well...I don't believe you."

"Believe what you want."

"$500 then. C'mon, help me out, dude."

"Bob," Harry said, looking Bob in the eyes.

"Fuck it," said Bob and Bob turned and walked away. Donna Fey, who worked in women's shoes, grabbed him and gave him a kiss. Harry didn't mind. It was a nice kiss.

"What was that for?" he asked.

"Hoping some of that luck of yours will rub off on me," Donna Fey said. "Believe me, I could use some luck."

He kissed her back.

"Well," he said.

"Call me," she said.

He'd asked her out once and she turned him down, just like Rachel.

"I will," he said.

"Will you?" she said.

"I will," he said.

"You promise?" she said.

"I promise," he said.

"I'll hold you to it," and she slapped him on the butt as he walked out of the store.

***

On the phone, at four in the morning, his cousin Pete said, "You and I, we had some times together, didn't we?"

"We have a bad connection," Harry lied. "Can you hear me? I'm having problems hearing you."

"Are you there? This is a *good* connection. I can hear you just fine. *Just fine.*"

"Do you know what time it is?"

"Seven," said Pete, "the day is just beginning. A new day, another chance to get it right."

"In New Jersey maybe," Harry said, "isn't that where you live now?"

"Hoboken, baby," Pete said. "Oh no, you're on California time aren't you?"

"Yes," said Harry, "yes, I am."

"My bad. Did I wake you?"

"Not really," said Harry and this was the truth, he was having a hard time sleeping, dreaming about crocodiles chasing him through the streets.

"You sound…good," said Pete.

"What's up?"

"What's up, he says," and Pete laughed, "what do you think is up, my dear old now rich and famous cousin?"

Harry closed his eyes. "What do you do these days?"

"I drive a limo to pay the rent. I shuffle rich assholes around all day."

"But it pays well?"

"I think it would be good for you to listen to me, listen to my voice, hear me out, hear what I have to say, cuz your old cuz has the big ideas, he knows what is what. And I right, or am I right?"

"Well…"

"I have an investment idea, ol' cuz o'mine, I have an idea that is going to make you richer beyond your wildest dreams."

"I already am," Harry said, "or, well, I will be, I guess."

"You *guess?*"

"Um."

"This is no time for guesses, this is a time for action! Are you ready to hear me out or are you ready to hear me out?"

"Why are you calling me, Pete?"

"To say *hello,*" his cousin said sarcastically.

"Hello back."

"You're a funny one, cuz."

Silence.

"Cuz," said Pete.

"Pete," said Harry.

"Ziiiiin," said Pete, and Harry wondered if his cousin was drunk. "My life has been shit, but I have a feeling that can change now. For years now I've had this idea for a business. It's a sure thing. I tried to get backers but these idiots all just laughed at me. Well they didn't laugh in my face but I know what they were thinking. Do you know what I mean or do you know what I mean?"

"I think I do," Harry said.

"Hear me out, hear me out, I say to you: hear me out ol' blood relative."

"Okay."

Pete made his pitch and Harry had no idea what his cousin was trying to get at.

"Hello? Harry?"

"I'm here."

"So what do you think?"

"I'm not sure, exactly, what to - "

"It's a sure thing."

"I'll need to think about it."

"What's there to *think* about, huh? I say, what's there to think about? Men of success *don't think*, cousin, they *act* - and they act fast when a good thing comes their way."

All Harry could do, at this hour, was sigh in a drowsy way.

Pete said, "I would like an immediate answer."

"How much would you need?"

"Let's say half a million."

"Half?"

"Four hundred K. That's nothing compared to the motherload you're getting, huh? Am I right or am I right?"

"I'm going to have to think about this," Harry said.

"WHY?!?" Pete screamed. "DO YOU WANT ME TO TAKE THIS HOT IDEA TO SOME OTHER POTENTIAL INVESTORS?!?"

Harry held the phone away from his ear.

"I'M COMING TO FAMILY FIRST CUZ WE CAN MAKE SOME COIN HERE, CUZ! Harry? Harry? HARRY?!"

"I'm here."

"Talk to me."

"I am."

"That's *talking?*"

"I'm really not a man of action."

"Oh so that's it, that is it," Pete said, "that's it, huh, just give your old cuz the brush off, hm? Well, tell you what, tell you what: the hell with you and your, and your, what, your ATTITUDE. You know what? This is what's what: I'm gonna give your father a call, I'm gonna call my father and then your father to have a little talk, a talk about you, about the kind of shitty person you've become, Harry. Is this what your new fortunes have made you? Is this what you have become or is this what you have become?"

And Pete hung up. But called back. "Just one question. Did you pick your own numbers, or was it a Quick Pick deal?"

"Quick Pick," Harry said.

***

And that's what it was. He'd stopped at Tran Vo Liquor before going to see Isabelle, to pick up a pint of bourbon. He always needed a drink after visiting his ex-wife. At the liquor store around the corner, he noticed the Lottery Machine and thought what the hell.

"Give me five Quick Picks."

The little old Vietnamese guy who owned the liquor store nodded and took Harry's money.

"Good luck you. Nobody ever win here but somebody win someday, ah."

Harry was walking downtown looking for a home. His eyes rested on the Harbor Twin Towers, a forty-story twin condo high rise. A week later, he was living in a two point seven million dollar condo on the thirty-third floor.

On one of his days with Isabelle, he hired a limo and took his daughter to every shopping mall in San Diego. He told her she could buy any clothes, toys, dolls and games she wanted.

"Anything and everything," he said, "the world is yours."

Isabelle didn't believe him but when she realized her father was serious, she started to scream like a kid and jump up and down like the kid. Sales people seemed to enjoy the eccentricity; other shoppers glared.

So.

Joanna wasn't happy either when the limo showed up stuffed with material possessions; it took half an hour for the driver, Harry and Isabelle to unload the stuff.

"How can you do this?" she asked.

"Because I can," he replied.

"Look at all this."

"She has good taste."

"What the *hell* are you doing?" She tried to keep her voice down. "What are you trying to turn her into? A spoiled little brat?"

"That won't happen."

"No? You want to spoil her. You want her to come to Daddy whenever she wants something and Daddy will *buy it all* with all his new bucks."

"This is a one-shot thing. I promise."

"I mean, it's not her birthday, its not Christmas, so what's the occasion?"

"Because it's today."

"You want her to love you more, is that it? Mommy can't buy what her heart desires, but Daddy can? When I say no, you'll say yes? Is that your plan?"

"No," he said. "Where's your sense of fun?"

"Where's *my* cut? Huh? Why does *she* get everything and I don't get shit? Tell me where the *fun* is in that, *Harry.*"

He didn't want to talk to his ex-wife.

"I'll make her take it all back, even if there are no receipts," she said.

"If you do," he said.

"*What?* What will happen, Big Shot?"

Harry smiled.

"I'll just buy it back again."

"You *would*," Joanna said, "wouldn't you?"

***

Security called and woke him up at nine a.m. They said the county sheriff was there and needed to see him. He wondered what happened. He was scared as he took the elevator down. He was not ready for bad news.

It was bad news but nothing devastating. The sheriff served him with a lawsuit. He was being sued by Tran Vo. Tran Vo owned the liquor store where he bought the lottery ticket. Tran Vo felt that because the ticket was purchased at his store, he was due 1/3 of Harry's winnings.

***

Harry woke up on a Wednesday around noon. He drank three shots of Knob Creek Kentucky Bourbon. With ice. He was with Joanna. They were just dating at the time and it wasn't serious.

She had been awake for a while. She sat in the bed next to him, playing with the remote on the TV.

MTV.

"Jane Says."

He hated Perry Ferrell.

"I don't want you to worry, but I'm late," Joanna said.

"Okay," he said.

"Did you hear me?"

"Yes."

They didn't say much after that. He tried to bring up something else; his job where they really seemed to like him. He tried to ask about her classes. She was still at the University. Studying anthropology. All the conversations fell into mumbling. He walked her back to her apartment. They didn't say much. All small talk. At the corner, he put his arm around her and told her that everything was going to be okay. Somehow everything would be okay. She didn't believe him; she let him hold her.

Three days later, she had her period. That was the first time Harry wanted to hear about a woman's period. They got married a year and a half after that.

***

A voice message from Alexia: "Harrison...Harrison...are you deliberately ignoring me, Harrison Mavin Evans? I think you are. I am convinced you are. Yes, I know you are. That is *not nice*. And what else is not nice? Let's see. You are blowing me off, I have a feeling, I know you are giving me the cold shoulder and I know you and your father are in cahoots. You are plotting and whispering behind my back just like the two of you did twenty years ago. I know what the scoop is, Harrison, and it's a scoop of poop. *How dare you.* I'm smarter than you are, and you know this is true! I'm smarter than you and your father both! You're both a couple of true bastards and I'm not going to take it anymore. I'll show you both what is what, I will."

Next: "Harrison? It's your mother. Yes, YOUR MOTHER. I may not have given birth to you like that dead bitch your father was once married to, that - that - WOMAN who popped you out of her dead uterus; but I raised you for the better part of your youth and I was like a biological mother to you and have been a real mother to you all these godawful years. So I have to ask, I have to ponder: how can a son treat his own mother the way you have treated me? You're a zillionare and you haven't given me squat. Except that hotel suite, what have I seen of our money? Yes, Harrison, OUR MONEY. WE ARE A FAMILY AND FAMILIES SHARE AND I WAS NICE AND RAISED YOU WHEN I DIDN'T HAVE TO SO YOU OWE ME, HARRISON, YOU OWE ME FOR ALL THOSE YEARS I LOST. Lost, yes, that's the word, lost. What have *you* lost, Harrison? *Nothing. Nada.* Is that fair? Is it? Harrison, IT IS NOT FAIR. I want you to give me what's mine, Harrison. I want my portion of your fortune so I can, finally, live the life I was meant to have. Keep acting stubborn, keep being the bad little boy, and you'll regret it."

***

He met Donna Fey for dinner at Jake's, a beachfront restaurant in Del Mar. It was the place she picked when he told her to choose one.

"The food is good and the setting is romantic," she said.

Romantic. Anything was possible; he could still feel her slap on his rear end. Donna was waiting for him in the bar. Black slacks, high heels and a bow tie at the neck of her blouse. Harry kept it simple with a gray sports coat and jeans.

"Am I late?" he asked.

"I came here straight from work," she said, "I'm on my second drink." She was holding a White Russian and Harry ordered one too. They toasted The Dude from *The Big Lebowski* and were shown to their table.

Chit-chat, banter and meaningless phrases. Harry was uncomfortable. He never knew this woman and she didn't know him. They didn't have any mutual friends so they started talking about the department store and then both agreed that was not a good topic. Donna said she hated the lack of direction in her life; she had no goals or desires because all she ever did was work.

"I have debts," she said; "I would like to go back to college and finish my degree and maybe go to grad school but I still owe on the other school loans so I couldn't afford school, I mean I'd have to stop working to go."

His mind was wandering, and so were his eyes; if he'd been paying attention he would have known what was going to happen next. Donna reached over and took his left hand and said, "Hey, are you here on Earth still, Mr. Evans?"

"Sorry."

"It's okay."

"It's not. I'm being rude."

"Are you okay?" she asked. "Something heavy seems to be on your mind."

She was drinking her fourth White Russian and still holding his hand. He watched one of her fingers stroke his palm but he didn't feel it.

He said, "I'm going to be blunt and say that maybe I should've just asked you to come see me at my home."

"And cut to the chase?"

"No chase."

"The capture?"

"The point."

"Which is?"

"How blunt do I have to be?"

"As *if,*" she said, tightening the grip.

"I didn't even ask if you were in a relationship, if you had a boyfriend," he said. "You see how rude I am?"

"I haven't asked the same."

"I'm here. I called."

"You called."

Two of her fingers were caressing him.

"*As* if," she said.

"As if what?"

"You're a funny man."

"Yeah, I should do stand-up comedy. Look."

"You look," she said, "because I'm going to be 'blunt' with you too. I do have a boyfriend, but I can't stand his ass. You know him. Bob."

"Bob? Bob from the job?"

"He's still mad at you for something."

"You two...?"

"He's not my type, I know, but he caught me in a moment of weakness and he does make me laugh. But he also *annoys* me. It's been a short thing, three months tops, and I'm ready to break up with him. I'll do it right now. Give me your cell and I'll do it this second."

"For?"

"For *you*," and she reached over and took his other hand. "Hear me out, I know I'm going too fast but I like it fast. I'm going to be *blunt* too. I really need your help, Harry."

"Help?"

"As in financial."

"But of course," he said. He tried to pull his hands away but she wouldn't let go. He wondered if this appeared funny from another table, or if they looked like a couple in love having a deep and serious talk about life and the future.

"I'm stuck in my life and I can't see a logical way out," Donna said; she was very serious. "I'm forty thousand dollars in debt and I just don't see how I can ever pay that off, not doing the work I do. And I can't move on to something else, like going to college or just starting over in another city. What I'm asking...what I want to offer...look, what I need from you is forty-five grand or so. That's chump change to a guy loaded like you are but for me, it's salvation, it's an end to my terrible burden. Now, hear me out, all right? I can't believe I'm actually doing this, but I'm buzzed and I am desperate. I'm prepared to make you a good offer. In exchange for that money, I will be your slave for six months. I don't mean like sex slave - but we'll have all the sex you want. I mean, I will always be on your arm, I will be devoted to you. I might even love you. You'll never have to be lonely because I will be there. I will be your constant companion, your soul mate, your best friend, your sister, your mother, your daughter, your pal, your wife. I can see it in your eyes; it's lonely at the top but you don't need to be a solo man. If you help me, I'll help you."

"And after six months, then what? Do I need to give you another forty thousand?"

"After six months, we'll see where we are."

He said, "Please let go of me...please."

She did. She sat back in her chair, sipped her drink and played with a strand of hair.

"I know I'm hot," she said, "I know I'm making you a pretty fine offer."

"What is it with you people," Harry said. "It never ends. Everywhere I turn. It's a wonder I ever step outside. I could be a total recluse and the phone would still ring. I could change my number but somehow people would find the new number. I never answer the phone because I'm afraid of what the person on the other side wants from me. And what do they want? Money!"

His voice was rising. Patrons at other tables were glancing over.

"Sure does make the world go around, doesn't it? Can I blame you? Should I? Would I do the same thing? It's always worth a try. You wouldn't give me the time of day a year ago but now that I can save you, now that I can bail you out, you are willing to whore yourself out for six months. And you know what? It's tempting. You're attractive, I've fantasized about you before, and yes, I am a lonely man. I'm a lonely man because I don't know who to trust. But I'm not surprised, not at all; I'm not surprised when complete strangers ask for - and demand money. Strangers are one thing. Family is another. No one thinks I deserve it. Since I won it and didn't work hard for it, it's not really my money."

Harry looked at her to see if she was angry. But she just stared at him with that same stupid look that was supposed to seduce him.

"Let me tell you about some of the people who want pieces of me. There's the Vietnamese fellow who owns the store where I bought my lotto ticket. He tried to sue me but the court dismissed the suit because there was no legitimate claim. In court this guy loses it, starts coming after me, telling me I better give him 'his' money, that's HIS money or else he'll come into my bedroom one night and slit my throat. The bailiffs had to take him away and he did two weeks for making a criminal threat in front of a judge. But did that stop him? No. He sent me letters demanding *his* money or else. Then there's my stepmother, who thinks she deserves something for acting like my real mother. Then I got cousins and aunts and uncles; people who claim they went to elementary school with me, they all have their own needs and stories. So I ask myself: why don't I give them what they want? I'll give it to them and be a saint and they'll be happy and I can be left alone. Maybe they'll come back for more, but so what? So what. It's only money. I'm still the same guy when I didn't have it, only now I can wine and dine at a nice place like this and not worry how much of my paycheck it's taking away. Don't look at me that way, Donna."

"What way?"

"Like I'm about to cut you down, because I'm not. And there's no need to say you're sorry or you didn't mean it because you did mean it and you're not sorry. I don't hold it against you. I understand. This is why I have decided the hell with it. I'm going to answer your prayer."

He pulled out his checkbook from inside his sports coat.

"I'm going to wash away your debts. How do you spell your last name?"

She told him. He wrote the check out for $45,000, and handed it to her.

"Are you playing a joke on me?" she said.

"Did you think I'd say no?"

Her hand was shaking as she held the check and looked at it.

Harry stood up and said, "And it's a gift. I don't want anything in exchange. You don't have to be my slave; you don't have to fuck me. You don't have to see me at all."

He put two one hundred dollar bills on the table.

"That should cover the bill plus a good tip. Have another drink or two, take a cab home, congratulate yourself on obtaining your goal, and go start your life over."

He left her with her mouth hanging open like she'd witnessed a horrible car crash. In the parking lot, Bob was waiting for him.

"So," Bob said, "dating my woman, are you?"

Bob had a pistol and was pointing it at Harry.

"I followed her, Harry, because I knew she was cheating on me. But with you? YOU? Do you think you can take anything you want because you're rich? And you give her all that money but wouldn't give me a few bucks?"

Bob shot Harry in the chest three times and Harry fell down and died.

Well, no, that's a lie, that didn't happen; Harry just imagined it. He thought about how funny that would be, if it did happen, if things were only that exciting. Nothing happened to him that night. He drove home alone.

He was hoping Donna would do the noble thing, the moral thing; that she would mail the check back to him with a note: *I can't take this. It's not right.*

He called the bank three days later. Customer service informed him that she had "cashed the instrument in question."

***

On voice mail: "Harrison? Are you there? It's your *mother*. I think you are there and you are ignoring me once again and, well, this is a horrid thing. Simply appalling. What kind of man have you become, Harrison? *Not a man at all.* I'm not going to take this sitting still, Harrison. You should understand that. You must understand that you will have to pay for your sins. Who wants to do that? Redeem yourself and do it today. *Redeem yourself and start doing what you know is right and good."*

***

Harry met her on the street in downtown.

"Hey," she said, and she was smiling, "how are you doing?"

They were both on Fifth Avenue walking in opposite directions. She was going to work and he was heading home. He thought maybe she recognized his picture from the papers when he won the jackpot, because he didn't know who she was.

"You don't remember me?" she said. "Kinko's. Seven or eight months ago. You were bleeding. Those are things you don't forget. At least I don't. Ha ha."

She had pink hair then; it was green now.

"Oh yes," he said, "yes, of course."

"You doing okay?" she asked.

"I'm doing...good," he said.

"That's good," she said.

"You still work at…?"

"On the way now," she said, walking, looking back, "I'm late, always late, I'm never on time. See ya."

Her name was Denise McNamara. The next few weeks he crossed paths with her again and they said hello. The third time he offered to buy her lunch.

"My lunch break is at 1:30," she said, "meet me?"

He did. They had pizza slices. She had no idea about his money. She wanted to know about that night he came into the shop bleeding.

"I drove into a tree," he said.

"Drunk?"

"Preoccupied."

"Must have been something dire."

"It was," he said.

"Thank you for lunch."

"I'd like to buy you dinner," he said, "but..."

"But?"

"I'm too old to be asking you out."

She said, "That's silly."

He was ten years older.

He said, "Well."

"I never say no to food."

"Um."

"Or cute men," she said eating her pizza.

Dinner, movie, dinner, lunch, drinks, movie, dinner. That's the story. The first time they made love and slept in each other's arms, it was at her place, a very small apartment in a part of San Diego called North Park. The apartment came with a Murphy bed that folded out from the closet and the bathroom seemed to have been made for small people, something Harry always noticed about these places built in the 1940s. She had a black and white TV that received three channels, a parakeet in a cage and around five dozen pairs of shoes. She didn't own a car and took the Number 7 bus to and from work everyday.

"The public transpo here is awful," she said, "but the 7 runs every ten minutes all day so it's cool."

She was born and raised in Denver, moved to San Diego two years ago; drove in the car she'd had since high school, which died two days after her arrival.

"Why here?" he asked.

"I wanted to be close to the water," Denise said.

***

He didn't tell her about the money and, for some reason, she didn't ask where he worked. Denise would later say that she just assumed he had some crappy-ass job like everyone else in the world; that when they'd seen each other on Fifth Avenue he was going to work like she was (he was taking morning walks). Eventually, he knew he would have to fess up because "things" seemed to be getting serious.

"Can I tell you something, Harry?" she said one night as they lay on her Murphy bed. "I'll tell you, I think I'm in love with you. I don't think. I believe. I know I am, I feel it: I'm in love with you and I'm not sure if I'm happy or worried."

It had been a long time since Harry M. Evans heard those words - not since Joanna, a year before he married her. Ten years ago. When he was Denise's age.

Denise said, "Is this okay?"

He said, "Yes it is."

"Cool," she said. "That night you came into my work…if someone told me this would happen, I would have laughed. I don't mean it's funny, this; I mean it's funny how things work out sometimes."

"I love you too," he said.

"I already know this."

The next night they spent together, Denise said: "Something is kinda bothering me, Harry."

"And what's that?" he said and he tried to tickle her, because he was feeling very good.

"Stop it," she said, pushing his hands away, "I'm attempting to be grim here. Or glib."

"What? What?"

"Why don't we ever go to your place? Two months, we've been together; two months and I love you like crazy and I have no idea where you live."

"You've never asked."

"Like I'm supposed to? Mister..."

"Come here," and he tried to tickle her again.

"Are you ashamed of where you live?" she asked. "I would understand."

"Let's go to my place then," he said.

"Right now?" she said.

"Right now," he said.

They took a taxi. The taxi parked in front of the Harbor Twin Towers. The night was chilly and there was smoke in the air. Something is burning, Harry thought.

"Why are we here?"

"You'll see," Harry said with a sad smile. Why sad? He was sure she would be mad at him, break up with him; he figured that day would happen no matter what, so why not now? Let the pain come home, he figured, let it happen now and not later.

"We can't go in here," she said in a small voice, *"rich people* live here."

Something inside him died and he shrugged.

"Harry," she said.

"It's all right," he said.

In the lobby, the two night security guards, wearing dark blue suits and red ties, stood up from the bank of video monitors.

"Good evening, Mr. Evans," they both said.

"Evening, Joe...Frank," Harry said, nodding and smiling and putting his arm around Denise's shoulder. "This is Ms. McNamara, she'll be going up with me tonight."

Both guards nodded, smiled at Denise and said, "Good evening, Ms. McNamara."

She said, "Hi," and hid behind Harry.

One of the guards turned the proper key to open the elevator doors.

"Harry?"

"We'll be there in a minute."

"I don't understand."

"You will."

They got off on the thirty-third floor and he took her home.

"Home," he said.

Denise looked around, walked around, stopped at one of the window and stared down at the city like a tourist. She sighed and put her hands on her hips.

"You like?" he asked her.

"What's the story," she said. She turned and glared. "Harry? This is weird. I mean, *this* is weird."

"I live here," he said. "I own this."

"Ha ha," she said.

"Yeah," he said.

"You're serious," she said.

"Yeah," he said.

"Oh, come on; are you house sitting?"

He told her about the lottery.

She said, "Whoa."

She said, "Why didn't you tell me before?"

She said, "Why didn't you *say* anything?"

"I'm not sure."

"You're 'not sure'?"

"No."

"Bullshit."

"I can't explain it," he said. "I wanted to tell you, but it didn't seem important."

She hit his left arm with her small fists and it hurt.

"That's crazy."

"I know."

"People brag about this shit."

"I know."

"And all this time...after all this time...you had me thinking..."

"I didn't want you to think anything," Harry said.

"I thought you were," she said, "I thought you some regular guy."

"I'm the same guy," he said.

"No, no," she said, "no, you are not."

"Don't say that."

"Ugh."

"Look."

"Did you think I would judge you?"

"I was just waiting for the right time."

"Oh Harry," Denise said and she turned to the window and played with her green hair.

"Are you mad at me?"

She laughed and shook her head and tugged at the hair.

"You are," he said.

"I'm not mad," she said. "I don't know what I am."

"You could be happy," he said.

"I could, I guess."

"You should."

"Why?"

"Because you love me."

"Well, yeah."

"Yeah?"

"Yeah, there's *that,*" she said.

***

The sun in his eyes; it woke Harry up. Denise was sitting on the edge of the bed, the sheets wrapped around her lightly freckled skin like a cape.

He said, "Hey."

She said, "Morning."

He touched her leg. "What's wrong?"

"Did you dream?" she said. "I had a lot of dreams."

"What did you dream about?"

"My father."

An awkward silence sat between them.

"I was thinking about him now," she said, "and all his crazy-ass ways. He was obsessed with winning the lottery. When I was growing up, he played it every week and that's all he ever talked about. All he talked about was - was how life would be different when he 'won it big.' When he'd get those millions. A new house, new cars, all the clothes I wanted, everything in the world. When I was nine, I believed him. I believed every week that he would win and I would dream about all the things he could buy; I would tell other kids my dad would win the lottery soon. I mean, he played all the time and people did win so the odds were good that one day he would win. 'This week is my week, I can feel it,' he would always say. And when he didn't win, he would get dark; he would drink; he drank a lot and got mean. He'd yell and cuss and hit my mother."

"Did he hurt you?"

"No. Never."

"You can tell me."

"No."

"Tell me."

"It was never like that."

"Is he still alive?"

"He's alive, and he still plays every week, talking up his stupid promises. This is why I hate the idea of lotteries. Everyone can't win. Everyone dreams they do. People play all their lives and they never get crap. It's not fair. Tell me, were there special numbers you picked?"

"No. Random, done by the computer."

"My dad plays the same numbers, the same goddamn numbers for fifteen years. He's convinced those numbers are bound to come up sooner or later. Tell me, Harry," she said, turning around, "have you done anything good with this money?"

"Good?"

"Right," she said.

Harry bought Denise a new car, a Hyundai, and she didn't say no. He wanted to give her all the things her father had promised year after year. Clothes, jewelry; he said she could quit her job and he'd take care of her forever.

"Forever is a long time," she said. He asked if she wanted to live with him in his castle in the sky; Denise did not give him an answer but she did pack up her possessions and took them to his condo.

"What do you *really* want?" he asked her.

"What can your money do to make me happy?" she said. "Is that what you mean, Mr. Harry Evans?"

"Yes," he said.

"What a question."

"Tell me."

"What if you don't like the answer?"

"I'll like any answer," he said, sounding like a man very much in love.

"Well," she said, acting like she was thinking: a finger to her chin, her eyes looking up.

"Well," he said, pulling her to him and kissing her cheek.

"Give some of it to the homeless shelters," she said, "to people who need it more than I do."

"Okay," he said.

"Yeah?" she said.

"Yes," he said.

"Awesome," she said.

***

One day, Harry took Denise and Isabelle to La Jolla Shores; they walked around on the beach and through the big rocks and looked at the sea lions lounging on the sand. It was the first time his girlfriend met his daughter. It was the first time that Harry realized that his girlfriend was only fifteen years older than his child. He felt suddenly old.

The two got along; they laughed and giggled and whispered and gave Harry funny looks.

"*I hate her,*" Joanna said on the phone, "I hate her and I want you to get rid of her."

"Where do you get off?" said Harry. "Where do you get off saying something like that to me?"

"I have *every* right."

"You're crazy."

"Don't call me that!"

"You are! What else is there to call you?"

"She's around my daughter," Joanna said, "and *that* gives me the right. She's a bad influence."

"You don't even know her."

"I don't need to."

"Did Isabelle say something bad?"

He listened to Joanna's breathing on the other end.

He said, "Well?"

She didn't say anything.

He said, "Isabelle said all good things. Isabelle likes her. They get along magically. So that's it; that's it, isn't it? You're threatened."

"Fuck you," said Joanna, "why would I bother?"

"That's what I wonder. Why would you care? It's not like Denise is taking your place; it's not like we're ever going to get back together."

"Fuck you, Harry."

She hung up.

She called back thirty seconds later. He knew it was her.

He said, "Joanna..."

"I hear you're giving money away left and right." She said, "You're just a regular saint, aren't you?"

***

"I feel bad," said Denise. "I've never met her..."

"It's nothing. She's just venting."

"So can I ask," Denise asked, "why you don't give her any money?"

"She doesn't deserve it," he said. "Do you think I should?"

"I don't know. What about your daughter?"

He told her about the $5 million trust he'd set up through his lawyer.

"She won't get the full amount until she's twenty-one."

He took his daughter out for dinner and she said, "Daddy, I want to live with you."

"What's going on?"

"I don't like living...with Mommy anymore. I don't. Can I live with you?"

"What's going on?" he said. "What's wrong?"

"She's always mad, she's always yelling," Isabelle said. "It's like she's going crazy or something."

***

He had to deal with the lawsuit; it was bogus, of course. Tran Vo just wanted an easy settlement, which Harry wasn't about to give. He had the money to hire the best attorneys in town, and seven weeks later the lawsuit was dismissed.

***

Isabelle was sick on one of the days he was supposed to have custody of her, so he went to see her. Isabelle was wrapped up in her blankets, in her bed, safe. He kissed her forehead.

"Daddy?"

"Yes."

"Can I come live with you yet? I don't want to live here anymore."

"We'll talk about that later, okay?"

"Daddy?"

"Yes."

"Can I have an ice cream cone? From our favorite place? I've been wanting one all day yesterday."

"I'll get you one right now."

"A double! Marshmallow and chocolate chip!"

Joanna was standing at the bedroom doorway, watching. She followed Harry. She stopped him, grabbed his arm; her fingers dug into his skin and that hurt.

"She's not going to live you with, ever. I want you understand *that*."

"Isn't it her decision?"

"No," Joanna said, "it's not."

"Please let go of me," he said, "please."

She didn't.

"You may be able to hire a dozen of the best attorneys in the universe," she told him, "but you will *never* have custody. You got that?"

"My turn...there's something I want you to clearly, and without a shred of doubt, comprehend."

"And what's that?"

"Isabelle will be moved in with me by the end of the month," he said. "This time, do the right thing. Just tell me what you want. I think I know."

"I want *money,*" Joanna said. "I'll need it to start over somewhere. A lot of money, you know…"

"You'll get it," Harry said, "and now, I have to get some ice cream."

"Get the damn ice cream," she whispered, "you get it and then we have arrangements to make."

She let go of his arm and he went out the door and walked down the street for two blocks and came to the ice cream parlor. Kids were sitting around, laughing and talking loudly and calling each other bad names.

He paid for two cones, one for him and one for Isabelle, and started to walk back. Someone from a passing car yelled, "YOU!"

The car was a beat-up Ford station wagon and the driver was Tran Vo, the liquor store owner. The station wagon came to a fast stop, tires screaming for vengeance.

"YOU HAVE MY MONEY! YOU GIVE ME MY MONEY!"

"Well, shit," said Harry, and he knew there was nothing he was going to be able to do.

Tran Vo jumped out of his car, brandishing a screwdriver. He approached Harry, yelling something in Vietnamese.

"I'm not in the mood for this," Harry said.

"YOU GIVE ME TEN MILLION DOLLAR NOW!"

"Take a hike."

"YOU HIKE ON THIS!" and Vo raised the screwdriver and lashed out, plunged, and swiped.

And then it happened. He was being stabbed first in the neck, then in the arm; then twice in the chest and once in the stomach.

He was lying on the sidewalk, bleeding like a broken fire-hydrant. He'd dropped the ice cream cones. Vo dropped the screwdriver, pointed at Harry and said: *"This all your fault!"*

Vo returned to his station wagon and drove away.

Harry lay there and figured this was it. He looked at the sky. Some kids from the ice cream parlor stood over him and they gawked and pointed with all the expected morbid curiosity.

"Is that *real* blood?"

"He's *bleeding* all right."

"Why did that other man stab him?"

"That's *not* real blood!"

"Eww, it is!"

Harry tried to say help.

Next, Joanna was kneeling next to him, touching his forehead.

"Harry?" she said.

"Hey," he said.

She picked up the screwdriver. She looked at the bloodied point, then at him. He forgot about her blue eyes. They were always so piercing.

She said, "I should finish you off," placing the screwdriver above his heart. "Isabelle would inherit all your money."

"Okay," he said, "do it."

"I'll have control of that money, all of it."

"Just do it," he said, *"do it."*

And so she did, plunging the screwdriver into his heart and killing him.

Well, no, that's a lie. He imagined she did that, and what would happen. She was probably having that fantasy, too.

His ex-wife reached into his pants pocket and found his cell. She called 911.

"They're on the way," she said.

"The ice cream," he said. "Isabelle…"

"Oh *Harry,*" she said, "you *just* don't *get* it, do you?"

In the paramedics van, hooked up to an IV drip, he asked, "Am I going to die?"

One paramedic said, "None of your major arteries were punctured; this is a good thing. What the hell happened to you?"

The other paramedic said, "You'll make it. You're a lucky man."

Harry said, "I'm a winner."

Michael Hemmingson lives in Southern California. His previous books include *The Naughty Yard* (Permeable Press), *Wild Turkey* (Forge), *The Rooms* (Blue Moon), *Comfort and Motion* (Olympia Press), *Star Trek: A Post-structural Critique* (Borgo Press) *Zona Norte* (Cambridge Scholars) and *William T. Vollmann: A Critical Study* (McFarland) among others. His first feature film, *The Watermelon*, was released summer 2009 and his short documentary, *Life in Zona Norte*, screened at the 2009 Cannes Film Festival.